SO-BRN-663

RL. A.'

ARThs 6.'

RL: 4.6

AR Pts: 6.0

ALSO BY GEORGE SELDEN
WITH PICTURES BY GARTH WILLIAMS

Chester Cricket's Pigeon Ride
Chester Cricket's New Home
The Cricket in Times Square
Harry Cat's Pet Puppy
Harry Kitten and Tucker Mouse
Tucker's Countryside

THE OLD MEADOW

GEORGE SELDEN

The
Old Meadow

ILLUSTRATED BY

Garth Williams

NEW YORK

FARRAR, STRAUS AND GIROUX

Text copyright © 1987 by George Selden
Pictures copyright © 1987 by Garth Williams
All rights reserved
Library of Congress catalog card number: 87-042950
Published simultaneously in Canada by Collins Publishers, Toronto

Printed in the United States of America
First edition, 1987

TABLE OF CONTENTS

THE OLD MEADOW

Dubber

"Here he comes again!"

Walter Water Snake craned his head up as far as he could above the surface of Simon Turtle's Pool. He could see just over the rim of the bank of luscious mud that surrounded, on three sides, the neat inlet where he and Simon lived. The fourth side opened out to the brook which in its rush kept fast fresh water circling their blue-green home.

"I'm gonna bite that mutt!"

"No, you're not," said Chester Cricket wearily. He'd heard all this before. Chester, too, lived in Simon's Pool—or rather above it, in a hole in a log that had been chewed out by Simon and Walt. The cricket's first home, a comfortable stump, had been squashed by two overweight ladies who sat on it. "You know you don't bite."

"I can try!" Walter fumed. "After all—I *am* a snake! And I have to keep up appearances."

"Walt—will you behave?" demanded Chester. "And not even pretend to bite Dubber?"

The Old Meadow

"Oh—*tchoor!*" When Walter Water Snake was feeling frisky, which was most of the time, or feeling mischievous, which was most of the rest, he said "tchoor" for "sure." The joke of life delighted Walter: how things and words could pop up so spontaneously, just the way he himself liked to pop up his head from the tranquil surface of Simon's Pool.

"Besides," wheezed Simon Turtle, "anybody who bites that dog runs the risk of mange." The old turtle had been spread out on his bank, drowsing and dreaming of how nice the world would be if it was all made of water and mud—with some sunshine thrown in, of course.

And indeed it was a lovely morning, a sunstruck morning, and the clear air seemed to ring like a bell. A wind like a steady invisible hand with a brush was combing the rich green grass of the meadow all one way. But through the beautiful summer day tramped a sad fat dog. His coat was knotted, there were burrs in it, two ragged bedraggled ears hung down, and his eyes were red and watery, as if he'd been up all night worrying—which he had.

"Hi, Dubber!" called Walter cheerily. "Hi, Rub-a-Dub-Dubber! You dapper and delightful dog!"

" 'lo, Walt," the dog grunted. " 'lo, Simon, 'lo Chester." He flopped down on the bank.

Simon Turtle and Chester Cricket each called as cheery a "Hi!" as they could.

4

"How *are* you?" Walt clapped the pool with his tail. "You live-wire fireball hot-ticket you!"

"I'm none of those things," said Dubber Dog. "I wouldn't set fires—honestly, Chester," he added apologetically.

"Don't worry, Dubber—I'm sure you won't," answered Chester Cricket. In his voice there was sympathy and an insect's tenderness, something tiny but real and very precious. It was always in his chirp, too. "How's Mr. Budd?"

"We're not so good." Dubber Dog was a mongrel, and there must have been some spaniel in him—as well as a breed with a tendency to put on weight. The spaniel came out in his ears. "As a matter of fact, we're getting worried and worrieder."

"Dubber—your *ears!*" said Walt. "They're hanging over into the mud."

"Who cares?" sighed the dog. "Mr. Budd won't notice. That's how worried he is. He doesn't bother to wash me now."

Walter Water Snake sank, and slowly sank farther, until just his eyes showed above the pool. He stared hard, in both annoyance and pity, at the dog sprawled above him on the bank.

"Were those men there again?" asked Chester.

"Yes," groaned the dog. "Four this time!"

"Well, they may not have been from the Hedley Town Council—"

6

"They were, though. They used all those words—'unsightly' and 'undignified' and—what was that new word—'deplorable'! I don't even know what that means, but it sounds very awful to me."

"It is," said Chester.

"One even said, 'This wretched little cabin lowers the tone of the whole Old Meadow. It definitely takes away from the charm.'"

"What a jerk!" sputtered Walt.

"Yes, and Mr. Budd threatened to bop him with our broom. But since it broke in half last week, I don't think that would have done much good."

"Did Mr. Budd whop you?" asked Walter very seriously.

"Of course he did. When they'd gone. Who else has he got to whop? Besides, he doesn't really mean it. Most times."

"That's no excuse—!"

"Oh, Walter, shush!" said Chester Cricket.

Walter tried to growl his disapproval, but his *rrrr* came out *ssss*, since he was a snake. He vanished below and cooled his temper in the soothing depths of Simon's Pool. Then just his two eyes appeared again.

"Walt, you don't understand," Dubber Dog explained. "Mr. Budd is afraid. Beneath those bushy white eyebrows of his and behind his beard—he's scared to death." Dubber's worry, the formless gloom of a blobby dog, was left hovering in the summer air.

7

His friends couldn't see it, but all of them felt it. These days it followed him everywhere.

Chester tried to stir up the sticky silence. "Well, but no one said anything like 'eviction.' Or that the Town Council would vote to tear down his cabin."

"Not yet." Dubber's voice, like his chin, slumped over the bank, down into the mud.

"Well, have hope! Have hope!" squeaked the cricket. "Right. Walt—?"

"Tchoor! Have hope." Walter Water Snake's hope was so weak, however, that he slumped back and sank.

"If they did throw him out, and pull down his cabin," said Dubber, "and put him in an old-folks home—it would kill him. I know it. He'd die. But not before he tore that old-folks home apart."

"That's what I'd do," said Simon Turtle.

"And as for me"—Dubber sighed, as only a pot-bellied mongrel can sigh; the depths of it came from the springer in him—"I'd just become a dog of the streets. They'd never take me back in Puptown."

"I knew it," muttered Walter, whose eyes were flashing on the surface again. "Puptown. Also known as Puppyville."

"Shhh!" Chester Cricket creaked under his breath. His glance at Walter was charged with meaning. It meant: Keep quiet—Dubber's very unhappy—and finally, Remembering sometimes lessens the pain.

"Puptown." Dubber's eyes gazed into the past, an

invisible space just before a dog's eyes. Then he chuckled, a rumbly kind of a sound that came out of his big old hanging belly. Chester Cricket didn't have any belly at all, but he always wanted to chuckle, too, when he heard Dubber heave up a laugh like that.

"Ah, Puppyville," said Walt, sighing. He leaned back on a wave like a rocking chair and prepared to hear Dubber's past. He'd heard it so often that after the first bit of repetition it almost seemed like a lullaby.

Simon, too, eased himself in the mud of drowsiness, and Chester shifted four legs to get more comfort from the noonday sun.

"I guess Daddy was a cocker or a springer," Dubber Dog began. His history relaxed him, too, since it was past and didn't hurt him too much now. "Mommy may have been a basset hound. But nobody knows. That's what Agnes thought. When I woke up the very first time, there was Agnes Fluger. And she was hovering over me. I'll never forget her." Dubber scratched one ear, very fast, with his right hind leg, the way a dog does, as if his memory, along with a flea, was in his ear and he might get it hopping with a good brisk scratch. "Nor will I forget her friend Marvin Detzinger, either."

"Nor will we," murmured Walt, as he rocked on the waves.

"Ag and Marv had this business which they called Puptown. They'd go all over Hedley and collect us

9

little leftover dogs and bring us home to sell to folks."
Dubber rumbled his deep bass, bubbly chuckle that
had to be called a belly laugh.

"That house was a sight! Pups tumbling everywhere." Dubber loved this part of the memory. "And
the television! I often heard her say while watching
soap operas, when someone had just killed someone
else, 'That lady just needs a little dog.' And the *ice
cream*—which she shared with us dogs, also while
watching television! That's when Puptown became
Puppyville."

"What *was* her favorite flavor?" asked Simon Turtle.
He'd lived a very, very long time and had only had ice
cream once. That was when a little boy named George
had dropped his Popsicle in the brook.

"Chocolate-caramel, as I remember, with hot-fudge
sauce. It drove her wild."

"I don't wonder," said Walt. "Myself, I'd never
risk it."

Dubber fondly scratched.

And suddenly Walter shouted, "Ugh!"—and ducked
beneath the surface. He came up spluttering with rage.
"Dubber Dog—I wish you would *not* scratch your
right or left ear beside this pool! I honestly do not
want to be remembered as the first snake in history to
come down with fleas!"

With a casual woof, Dubber brushed off Walt's fear,
if not the flea that had landed on him. "I was covered

with ice cream a lot, in those days. Because Aggie decided that I was her favorite."

"Sundae?" said Walter.

"No—dog. She shared all her goodies with me. Even cranberry sherbet, when that came out. And when people came who'd try to adopt me—in those days I really was quite—quite—"

"—the cutie!"

"I *was* nice, Walter Water Snake! But Aggie would say, 'Oh, no—that one's not for sale.' And then she'd feed me up on more mocha-raspberry-pineapple splits!"

"What a fate! Well—"

"So by the end of half a year I was unadopted and getting fat. But one day Marv came back from Big World of Cars, the garage where he worked in the day, and he took one look at me—I was sprawled on Aggie's living-room rug, lapping up praline ice cream from a pan and engrossed in a TV serial where somebody's mother eloped to Hawaii—and Marvin said, 'We've got to get rid of that dog. The older he gets, and the fatter he gets, the less likely he is to find someone to love him.'"

"Oh, that's so true," sighed Walter sadly. "Applies to snakes and people, too."

"Anyway," Dubber Dog went on, "Marvin said that otherwise—if I stayed fat and nobody got to like me— I'd have to go to the corner of Squigg Street and Lebel Avenue. And *you* know what's there! Even *I* knew what was there—at the age of six months." Dubber paused, to let the terror and awe sink in.

"*The dog pound!*" chorused Simon Turtle, Walter Water Snake, and Chester Cricket together.

Their doom-laden voices were just what Dubber needed to hear. "Yes! And right at that moment Mr. Budd came in and found me with my nose full of ice cream. Of course you field folk had known him before—"

"Lord!—for how many years," wheezed Simon Turtle.

"—but that was the first I'd seen of him. It was just after Jimdandy, his dog who ate boiled beets, had died, and he saw me with my jaws dripping ice cream, and he said, 'That's him! He needs me.' So that was it. I got adopted. But also, I secretly think inside—Mr. Budd is afraid of the pound himself. It was after a little talk with Marvin that he grabbed me up and rushed me away. To his cabin."

"He's kind of fat himself," said Simon. "Though Lord knows how he gets that way—just eating those scrawny vegetables."

"Our vegetables are *good!*" woofed Dubber Dog indignantly. "They're not scrawny!"

"How *did* you get used to vegetables?" wondered Chester Cricket. "After all that sweet ice cream? Must have been a big comedown."

"It took some doing," admitted the dog. "But you

know Mr. Budd: with a carrot in one hand and a beet in the other—he won't take no for an answer. Besides, I needed the vegetables anyway—to reduce after all that goo." He heaved himself into a new position. "Not that it did so much good."

"Tchoor—we know Mr. Budd," muttered Walt. "He whops you. Does that help to reduce you, too?"

"It doesn't mean he hates me," hoped Dubber. "In fact—that last day—he demanded of Aggie and Marv that they take a dollar bill. They had wanted to give me away—but Mr. Budd said, 'Nope, nope—he's my dog now. He deserves to be bought.' They compromised on a quarter."

In a stillness, the wind brushed Dubber's hair. For those who had no hair—like Simon, Walt, Chester—the wind felt like a smooth hand on their backs.

"So, Chester," said Dubber, "that's why I was wondering"—his voice drooped to a plea—"I was wondering if as Chester Cricket you might solve the problem—I mean, take away all the worry—about words like 'eviction,' and 'unsightly.' I mean—as applied to Mr. Budd's cabin."

"*Me!*" squeaked Chester. He'd known all along that the sadness of Dubber Dog would end up right on his wings. "Why *me*? I'm just a little cricket. Who sometimes has friends who help. Why me?" Chester's voice got swallowed inside his throat. "This is a big problem—"

"Sometimes," said Simon, "it takes a little, ingenious person to find his way through the holes of an enormous problem."

Iron worry imprisoned everyone.

"Did he whop you—hard?" Walt had to ask.

"Not really," said Dubber apologetically. He often had to defend his master before his friends.

"Oh—Mr. Budd," Walt moaned with sadness and anger and sorrow. He let himself sink.

"Oh—Mr. Budd," Simon, Chester—the whole Old Meadow—sighed back in echo.

TWO

Mr. Budd

Oh, Mr. Budd . . . Mr. Budd was the problem.

As the animals lingered beside the brook, they chatted together about the old man. Their talk drifted into the deep Old Meadow, a place that was fairly overgrown with the vines and the grass and the secretive flowers of Abner Budd's life.

"Scrawny vegetables! As if we'd ever raise such things!"

Of all the field folk, Simon Turtle understood the problem of Abner Budd best, although the two, man and turtle, had had, for over sixty years, just a nodding acquaintance. Long before Dubber or Chester or Walt had been born—and in fact just after he himself had come out of the egg—Simon Turtle had known about Abner Budd. And the man's life had grown to be entwined with the fate of the whole Old Meadow. He was the single and—as he liked to say—the 'onliest' human being to live there. That is, to live in the meadow since the farms failed, were sold, or the barns burned down. He was just something there, in his cabin, upstream, like the old gnarled tree that grew beside his vegetable patch. That tree dropped its leaves in the brook, and for years they'd sailed past Simon's Pool on their way to a river and then the great sea. But since Mr. Budd had gotten to be a problem—and no one knew how: he just *was*, one day—those leaves seemed to Simon like anxious notes. They'd been written by weather on an old willow tree and mailed by a brook, and each one was received by a worried old turtle. His fear had been very slow to grow, like his legs heaving up the bank or his head as he craned around, but it got there, fear did, just where it was headed—deep into his heart. Turtles get where they're going.

"The lettuce is especially lovely this year."

"Oh, Dubber—*drat*! By my shell—we've got something much more important than vegetables to think about!"

The Old Meadow had a great, deep past. Simon's forebears were the only field folk who remembered its whole long history. Farmer Hedley had been the first to live there, and love that land that the brook ran through, and cultivate it, and make it a farm. He'd made peace with the proud Indians who lived thereabouts in Connecticut, and in exchange for services, like medicine when they were sick, they'd sold him the Old Meadow. In fact, that tribe—the Sistikontik— had liked him so much that they'd helped him pile the boulders and stones of his new property into a splendid natural wall. It still could be seen, if a field person or a human being had the eyes for such things. Beneath the ivy and shrubs and the clinging wildflowers that the years had encouraged, there the stone wall stayed. One eager crimson morning-glory vine had rioted over half a mile. But those stones were well laid. Though tumbled in places, they seemed to remember the hands that had put them where they belonged. And they were as faithful to the farmers who worked as a turbulent nature—wind, rain, snow—would allow.

Farmer Hedley sold out to a man named Santell, and Andrew Santell left the farm to his son-in-law, rich Phillippe LeBel, a French Canadian who'd come down from Quebec. Phillippe's son, Edmund, came back every Saturday night quite tipsy from the local tavern, the Cow Lick, so the farm and the meadow went again to a son-in-law, Paul Squigg. Edmund, by the bye, went to California to search for gold—and never discovered as much as a nugget. The Squiggs had the land for two generations, doing middling well, but the last Squigg, Simon, bred a new kind of corn and made a fortune. He sold—and this was a gloomy sign—to someone who didn't live where he farmed. His tenant farmer—named

Pett—did all he could, but it wasn't enough. Edward Stroke, who'd bought from the Squiggs, just wanted land. He was greedy, and felt he was rich just if he owned earth, brook, trees—even tuffets. And Edward Stroke the Second, his son, was even more careless of land. He'd found that even owning it and doing nothing was profitable. You just had to wait till there wasn't enough land to go around—and then you sold out, and were rich. So for two generations, father and son, the earth, raw soil, didn't do a thing, except play. Weeds grew—and trees—the bushes went wild— hidden flowers flourished, which no one saw. The stone wall was covered by layers of years. The Old Meadow stood still—in the heart of the state of Connecticut—uninhabited, wild, so everyone thought.

But everyone was wrong.

"And the beet greens are marvelous!—this year."

"Oh, beet greens! Oh, *beet greens!* I must retire below."

The Old Meadow was inhabited, and not only by the field folk, although the field folk knew more about the man who was living there than any human being did.

Edward Stroke the Second, along with the Old Meadow, had inherited a lonely soul. And this neglected human being was just as alive—and just as determined to stay alive—as the wild morning glories that covered the old stone wall.

"Mr. Budd is also inventing a new kind of squash this year."

"Oh, really?"

"Yes! And Walter, don't you laugh! Snakes could learn to like squash, too."

"*Oh*—boy."

Mr. Budd had become, at the age of sixteen, a success in the Old Meadow. This was his only happiness, since he knew that outside Tuffet Country, Pasture Land, the brook—outside his green world—he was a failure.

He'd always been a loner, but never by choice. Few people are. And, at sixteen, to be a loner hurts. Abner Budd was sixteen when he ran away. His parents had died when he was so young that about the only thing he remembered was milk. He'd been taken in by a well-meaning neighbor, a single man with a crippled arm, who tried for years to do his best by the boy. But in those days, which were years in the past, most people felt that whopping a boy was how you made him learn to behave. Also the neighbor—his name was Paul Santelle, and he owned a little delicatessen, and he was quite nice, or at least he wanted to be—Paul went to the principal of the school where Abner was studying, and the principal said, "Keep him in line!" That meant *whop!* when necessary.

Abner Budd, at sixteen, decided that it was no longer necessary. And he got only one whopping more. This one, strangely, did what the other whippings hadn't; it gave him a sense of right and wrong. He'd run off and hidden himself in the Meadow. Farmer Pett, the last who lived on the land, found him sleeping beneath the bushy vines on the east side of the wall. It was August, and Abner had planned to eat some corn— raw. When Pett heard that, he decided that he'd been whopped enough. After lunch, after dinner, Abner ended up as the hired hand of Luke Pett.

Luke grew to think of Abner as kind of a wild son, an accidental gift like the irises the Old Meadow gave him every year. Those were happy years for Mr. Budd, who wasn't Mr. Budd as yet. He was "Abner" or "Ab" or "Kiddo" when Luke was in an especially good mood. Happy years—the happiest in the boy's life. He found that he really did like farming; he liked Luke Pett very much—and most of all he liked not getting whopped anymore. But the years of feeling like a family, if only a thrown-together one, didn't last very long. In the very month of Abner's twenty-first birthday, Luke Pett got killed by an oil truck that went out of control on Mountain Road. That afternoon, with its sudden emptiness which the boy felt within his heart, may have been the day when Abner turned into Mr. Budd, the cantankerous character of the Old Meadow.

The Old Meadow

It didn't help either, that same afternoon, that Edward Stroke appeared on the scene and told Abner he was fired. As long as his tenant farmer was gone, he was going to take a tax loss on the whole place. Just let it sit. He'd be glad if Abner was out in a week.

He was out in a night. He packed his few things from the room he'd fixed—a corner of the attic, hung with unused curtains and draperies, to make it warm and colorful—and rushed them all across the brook. He buried them, and the calendars, too. But after the cabin was built, they all were molded to earth, and not a single thing could be used. He'd run through the cornfield, the apple orchard, and settled down at last, like a thief—which he wasn't yet—in a far-off, hidden thicket in the northwest corner of the Old Meadow. No goodbyes—to anyone: there was no one to say goodbye to—and no words in his throat anyway. He ran.

And stay hidden two weeks. And now he really did become a thief. Stole apples from the orchard and whatever little vegetables he thought the Strokes wouldn't notice.

Mr. Stroke, who had chosen not to live there, put boards on the windows and locks on the doors, and the great homestead stood alone.

However, that farmhouse was not uninhabited. Mr. Budd, after two months of living beneath the trees and sleeping on pasture grass, ventured back—and pried open a cellar window. He made himself a bed of leaves and luckily found four moldy blankets. And for that first winter he lived on the vegetables—boiled in brook water—he'd been able to collect. The turnips helped, and the fire to cook them kept him warm, almost.

But he didn't dare make too much of a fire: someone might suspect that a human soul was living there, and finding his food in a meadow that had been let go.

That first winter was the worst: the coldest and the loneliest. Mr. Budd had to stay covered up by those blankets for days at a time. But he had no place to go. He was big enough now not to be whopped by anyone. But the trouble was—there was no one he knew! No one even cared enough to whop him now. Luke had gone—he'd always called him *Mister* Pett—and in all Abner's green, golden, snowy world there was no one he knew. Or knew him. Or he liked. And he *knew* that no one could ever like him. And in summer, winter—in spring and fall—in all the wide, terrifying world, there was only one place where he felt at home: the Old Meadow. Where he was alone.

The second year was much better. Abner ventured out of the sagging farmhouse, which creaked as the joints settled into each other, and got a few odd jobs around town. When anyone asked him where he lived, he just waved his hand vaguely, off toward the west, and said, "Oh, over there." Now he could buy a few necessary things, like a kerosene stove with a very low flame, and a couple of candles. But he didn't unboard the windows, because he knew he was really trespassing in somebody else's house. Even though that someone—those somebodies, the Edward Strokes, both senior and junior—could not care less about the fate of this old and beautiful, living home.

Still, every so often, from the roads all around the Old Meadow—and there got to be more and more of them—a light, a glimmer of yellow candle flame, could be seen from the boarded, blind windows. The farmhouse was thought to be haunted.

It was. By Abner Budd. At the vigorous age of twenty-one he'd become a ghost—a candle in an abandoned house. He was young and he was handsome, kind—at least all the animals thought he was, when he fed them in the winter. And sensitive: he could understand the many moods of the morning glories that bloomed along the old stone wall. He had black hair and a black mustache, which he kept trimmed as best he could with a knife. Scissors would have been very expensive, and he needed the money from mowing and painting, tidying up after other people, for kerosene and canned food for the winter. He was six feet two and very strong, from nature's kindness and working to keep himself alive. Above his mustache and a nose with a little ridge in it were gray-green eyes, which were thoughtful because he looked at the brook so much and wondered about its current. But sometimes those eyes

24

were frightened, too. Mr. Budd was afraid of the future and afraid of the world outside, by which he meant everything that wasn't the Old Meadow. Tall, strong, there was still something in him sixteen years old, despite Luke's efforts to grow him up. The love hadn't lasted long enough. So there Abner was: young, handsome, strong—and inside himself as worried as a chipmunk. For a long time he tried to trim his mustache, but after the waiting—maybe twenty years—when the first gray had splashed his hair, he gave up. No one would ever notice, he thought—neither him nor his face—and he gave up his cheeks to a scraggly beard.

"We have the best vegetables in Connecticut! And always have—since Mr. Budd began growing his own."

Meanwhile, between mustache and beard, a lot happened Outside.

The biggest thing was the Great Depression. When Abner first heard those words, from a younger man whose garage he was roofing, he thought that the earth might be sinking. It wasn't. But everyone's money was. The Strokes' money, too. They sold the farmhouse and all the acreage on the other side of the brook to be a driving range. Those words were also a mystery. Ab found out later it meant a golf course where no one played golf—just hit the little balls into nowhere to see how far into nowhere they'd go.

The Old Meadow

But, one morning, tractors and trucks and men were outside about to tear down the farmhouse. Shuttered up though he was, Abner Budd had begun to think of that house as his own—but it wasn't. That's all he could think of—"I have no home!"—as he gathered up his four moldy blankets, clean now they'd been washed so often, and dashed across the brook. From the other side he watched them demolish the farmhouse and start to smooth out the field for the range, so no little golf ball would ever get lost.

When he couldn't stand the sight anymore, he fled away, deep into the meadow. By fate, luck, or deep memory, he found himself in the very same spot he'd sheltered in five years before—the day he'd run away.

Abner had to act fast: build some kind of shelter. It was October. And although the various golds of autumn were a treasure in his heart, he knew what they meant: winter coming—beware! He patched together a rickety shelter on the safe side of the brook. But still it was a good beginning, like his love for Luke Pett. There were poplars all around; a giant oak hung over it; and a thick good hedge hid the driving range where little white balls were whacked nowhere.

On the first night of destruction, the farmhouse half down, Abner managed to sneak back to what had been home and salvage a few things: a kerosene stove, held high above his head as he managed the passage of the brook, those blankets and a load of vegetables from the

cellar. He thanked the stars that were out that night that no guards had been left to protect the trucks and tractors. The loneliness that he'd felt as a boy closed all around him again as he tried not to drop and drown the stove. But when he reached the stream's other side, a different feeling was waiting for him. It was freedom, a little bit of freedom, his own, contained in the wildness of an old meadow surrounded by roads and a busy town.

The shelter grew rapidly into a cabin. The kerosene stove held off the frost, and the first snow stayed where it should—outside. Mr. Budd borrowed stones from the tumbled stone wall to make a fireplace and chimney. Where they didn't fit they were held together by two dollars' worth of cement. Two dollars was quite a lot in the time of the Great Depression. Of course, most of the cabin was made of wood. Mr. Budd raced the wreckers—they ruined by day, he built by night— to salvage enough from the old farmhouse for the walls and the roof of a hidden little cabin. Glassine windows —that's something transparent, but unlike glass, it unrolls—could be bought for the price of an ice-cream cone. Mr. Budd's odd jobs helped a lot, in the earliest, anxious days. His favorite windows faced south and west—the strength of the sun and its glorious colors at sunset.

Most precious of all the things that Mr. Budd snatched from destruction—the farmhouse was almost

Mr. Budd

gone by now—was a three-legged stool. Luke Pett had made that stool. And he loved very much to sit on the work his own hands had done. He said the world looked better from there. It looked better to Mr. Budd, too. On a stoop of flat stones he'd built out in front of his only door, Mr. Budd sat on that stool, alone, and let the seasons pass through him. Spring, summer, fall— even winter. After a snowfall, a hard one too, Mr. Budd would bundle up in the raggedy clothes he stitched for himself, or people gave him, or he found in trash cans, and he'd sit, alone, in a world made white. Snow seemed like fate: it was everywhere. But then, in the air, a blue appeared which shone on the snow. It got brighter and brighter—in the sky, everywhere. Mr. Budd loved those hours most of all—although, unless he was well wrapped up, his teeth and his toes began to chatter.

Years passed. They all felt different—the leaves, the colors—but they all were the same—the brook and Mr. Budd.

Sometimes he cried, when the loneliness of an owl's hoot reminded his heart of something else. But often he laughed, like the time he saw a high-spirited squirrel chasing a rabbit in circles.

Mr. Budd knew he had to do two things if he was going to keep alive in this satisfactory cabin of his.

The first was—plant a garden! He knew a lot about gardening from his years on the farm. And he also knew where the seeds were kept—in a shed behind the house.

The Old Meadow

The wreckers got there last of all, and when they did—well, they wouldn't have known good seed from bad.

But Abner did. Tomatoes—all radiant red, and fat as babies, and solid little yellow jobs, but sweet as Popsicles. Squash, lima beans, peas—and string beans too, not Abner's favorites—but they all had a place. Abner knew how good green was. He decided he'd eat something green every day. But the other colors enticed him, too. Yellow squash—pale moon-colored melons—and best of all the red of beets!

Abner planted a garden.

The second of Abner Budd's adventures, which took more courage than planting seeds, was—he adopted a dog. The feeling of being by himself, when the blue came through the snow or the sun came from under a cloud in August, became unbearable. There had to be someone to share the splendors and sadness with.

The first dog he bought came from the pound. "I want one that's hopeless," he said. "I'll buy the one you can't get rid of. The runt." The name of the first was Ida, a strange mix of poodle and beagle. Then Roger, an even stranger combination of Afghan and bulldog.

Ida had—almost—liked peas. Roger put up with green beans. And the next one, Nate, ate broccoli stalks as if they were big green bones, with a wistful look that seemed to ask, 'You're not gonna take this away, are you?' For one thing these dogs had in common: they had to like vegetables. Those were all Mr. Budd could provide: the vegetables that he grew.

Mr. Budd

At first he'd say to the little puppy—"Come on now, try this asparagus," depending on the season. And he'd cuddle the puppy, as he waved a stalk under its nose. But after years, when his patience ran out, it was—"That's all there is! Eat squash or starve."

Both methods worked. And generations of mongrel dogs had been turned into vegetarians. Some did make Mr. Budd laugh too, which wasn't all that easy. Jimdandy did especially. He had a passion for boiled beets, and after a month or two Jim's muzzle was red as a ruby. Mr. Budd would roar every time he saw him.

But after Jimdandy got old, got fat, and finally got tired—even of beets—Mr. Budd gave up the pound. He didn't like the atmosphere there, and somewhere he heard about Puptown. Dubber was the runt in this case—a pretty fat runt—and Mr. Budd got him for twenty-five cents.

"And the escarole is so tasty this year."

At first, Dubber Dog had been afraid of vegetables. Since he'd mellowed out on chocolate ice cream and marshmallow sauce, peas seemed like a letdown to one fat runt. But there was something about that shack. Cabin, rather: Mr. Budd's home. The love of the dogs who'd lived there still lingered. And so did Mr. Budd's love for them.

"And speaking of escarole—"
"*Always* a challenging subject!"

31

The Old Meadow

"—the tomatoes are coming up lovely, too! So are Robert Rabbit's carrots."

"What does this have to do with *me*? I eat leaves! And occasionally a blade of grass."

"Don't fly off the handle now, Chester. But you did save the meadow—with those friends of yours from New York. Before, it was just a wild place—weeds, and trees whose roots were strangling everyone and each other. In those days Mr. Budd and his cabin were just some more wildness. No one noticed. But then you saved it, and paths were put in, and our shack became an 'eyesore.' "

"But 'twasn't Chester's fault."

"I know, Simon. But Mr. Budd isn't *safe* anymore. You field folks are safe. And the insects, too. And Mr. Budd loves you all. He's never, ever killed a spider. And Donald Dragonfly's his good friend. But in the old days—the overgrown days—he knew his place and expected you to know yours, too. Now even a skunk cabbage isn't safe. You're saved, all right—but not Mr. Budd. And, Chester—"

"*What—?*"

"Don't twitch your antennae! I know that means you're mad. Those men—from town—I heard them agree that at the very least our vegetable garden had to go."

"Oh, *vegetables!* I'm sick of that word!"

"You water snake! If ever you got hungry enough,

you'd eat a vegetable! Even those little green slimy things that grow at the bottom of Simon's Pool. Where you slip and slide!"

"I'd eat *dog*—in a pinch!"

"I'd eat you both!" shrieked Chester Cricket. "If it would stop you bickering!"

Luckily, something happened to interrupt the nasty fight that was thickening in the air. The unexpected is always welcome, but the beautiful is a gift. From upstream a melody came caroling down, as if afternoon had found a voice.

"What's that?" asked Chester, as the notes of the song flowed through his small chest, made it bigger and bigger inside its shell.

"Oh, him," said Dubber. "That's only our mockingbird."

THREE

Ashley

"*Your* mockingbird?" Chester tried not to hear the song for a moment, to concentrate on Dubber's answer, but his heart yearned for it to go on and on.

"Well, he's sitting on our cabin. He can be the Old Meadow's mockingbird, if you want. We've had them here before."

"But not one that sounded like *that*."

"When did he get here?" The cricket's curiosity tingled all along his antennae. "Where does he come from?"

"He flew in yesterday." Dubber Dog scratched, very casually, his long right ear. "And landed on our weather vane. Made J. J. Bluejay furious, too. He likes to perch up there and squawk. Mr. Budd threw a squash at him, though, when he tried to push the mockingbird off."

"Just skip all that J.J. *Ouch!*" Walter Water Snake had forgotten where he was, and whacked Chester's log by mistake.

Ashley

"Mr. Budd thinks the mockingbird is the greatest thing since maple syrup."

"So do I!" said Chester Cricket.

Dubber hung his head—then forced a chuckle. "It even makes me a little jealous, how fond of him he is."

"I've got to meet him!" Chester jumped from his log to the bank. "A musician like that—with such a voice—!"

"Hey, wait! Me, too!" Walter started to slither upstream.

"*And* me! But you people will have to go at my pace."

Simon Turtle's pace, which was measured by hours, not minutes, only added to Walter's and Chester's impatience. To quiet their fidgeting—one sloshing around in the brook, one hopping up and down on the bank—Dubber said, "You guys know how much Mr. Budd likes birds. Sometimes in winter he puts me on half rations so he can buy birdseed with what he earns from those odd jobs of his."

"Every little bit helps," huffed Simon, as he waddled along.

"How would you know?" Walter zigzagged and circled and did figure eights in the water. "Come winter and you're underground."

"Oh, I hear things," the turtle wheezed. "Either sooner or later—in spring mostly—a turtle learns the truth."

The Old Meadow

"Shh!" warned Chester. "We don't want to scare him."

As the four animals approached the cabin, the mockingbird's song grew gradually louder. There were shreds of the melodies of all the meadow birds in that song, but also—suddenly—wonderful musical phrases that poured from the bird's own imagination.

"Look! There he is!" Walter Water Snake saw him first, with his bright black eyes.

Mr. Budd's weather vane and Luke Pett's handmade stool were his most prized possessions. In ways, the weather vane meant the most: he'd bought it himself, thirty years ago, in an antique shop that was going out of business, with money he'd earned. It was a graceful iron bird, with wings extended, that always flew into the heart of the wind, as a weather vane always must.

Just now, on the left wing, there was perched a living bird made of flesh and feathers and thrilling voice. He was somewhat larger than John Robin, but not nearly as big as J. J. Bluejay. His back was gray, but the down of his underside was white, and he had white markings on his wings. An elegant yet not flashy tail seemed to complete him with a flourish. To Chester's eye, despite his size, he was even more lordly than the great metal bird he was sitting on. No iron or steel could ever release a voice like that. Mockingbirds, indeed, had appeared in the meadow before, but—but—the sound from this throat went up and down, as if it were only testing itself, just playing, for fun. In quick and liquid drops it trilled, striking two notes close together. And sometimes it held on to one pure tone—for a long and then a longer time—so long it could make a cricket's heart break.

"I've got to meet him!" sighed Chester almost fearfully.

"He's shy," said Dubber. "Very shy. Mr. Budd was trying to coax him down all morning."

"Where is the old geezer?" asked Walt.

"He's *not* an old geezer! And he's asleep. Inside. Because of our worry, he hasn't been sleeping too well this summer. But that mockingbird lulls him right off. And even in the afternoon—like today.

"I've got to meet him." Chester Cricket, in a faraway voice, seemed now to be talking almost to himself. His mind was saturated with music.

But then a thought interrupted his reverie. The mockingbird had just spun out a tone of five notes. Using his legs—they made the famous chicket's chirp —just as carefully as he could, Chester imitated the bird. He mocked a mockingbird, although there was nothing but awe and admiration in the sounds he made; no mocking at all. But then there was never any mockery in the sounds the bird made himself, no making fun of anyone. There was only a joy in the world he heard, and a wish to repeat its sounds again.

On the weather vane, the birdsong ceased. The

mockingbird seemed more than surprised: he was shocked to hear someone play *his* private song. He looked down, and his eyes swept the bank where the chirps came from.

"Well, I never—!"

And then, to Dubber's astonishment, he flew down —hovered above the animals—and alighted in front of Chester Cricket. "You did it, didn't you?"

"Now just a minute, Mr. Mockingbird!" Walter wriggled up swiftly from the brook. "You've got to promise not to eat up our cricket. We have the Truce in this Old Meadow. And Chester's special."

The mockingbird bowed slightly to the snake. "Don't worry, mah scaly friend—I never had a taste for good people." He turned back to Chester. "It *was* you, though—"

"Yes, sir, Mr. Mockingbird—" Chester Cricket was flustered. "But I wanted to meet you. And I couldn't think of anything else."

"Best chirpin' I've ever heard!" The mockingbird shook his head. Then laughed. Then whistled— *"Eee-ooo!"*—just like an astonished man. His laugh, too, was music, the kind a brook makes when it's rushing over stones, with someplace to go. "I've met mah match—an' no doubt about it!"

"Can I—can we—" began Chester. "Can all of us know your name?"

"It's Ashley. Ashley Mockin'bird. I'm proud to meet y'all."

Ashley

Chester introduced himself and his friends.

Ashley sang his private melody, the one that Chester had imitated. Without a word being spoken, everyone knew he was greeting them all as a friend: a mockingbird's way of saying hello.

The afternoon was growing old. Sun shone through torn clouds like fragments of floating cloth. Yet a sudden excitement filled the day, seemed to sparkle on the brook. It was as if the Old Meadow woke up: who *is* this new person?—and, something's different now! The excitement got difficult.

Chester Cricket spoke into the silence. "Do you come from far, Mr. Ashley?"

"From West Virginia," said Ashley Mockingbird. "I've spent mah whole life, so far, in the hollers of West Virginia."

"A holler?" said Walt. "I thought a holler was when someone yelled at you."

"Why, no," said Ashley. "In West Virginia we have these wonderful up-and-down mountains. Big trees and bushes, and ten-times-ten kinds of flowers—like what y'all enjoy hereabouts, but wilder, maybe. And in between two green mountains, with a creek flowin' through it, most likely—why, that's a holler. There's often a secret openin', an' once you get through it, a sweet valley stretches ahead of you—for animals, birds, human bein's too, to live in an' make their home."

"I think he means 'hollows,'" whispered Chester politely. "Folks live in hollows, in West Virginia."

"That's what I said"—the mockingbird let loose a daring song—" *'hollers'*!"

At the questioning of his new friends, Ashley Mockingbird explained how he happened to be in Connecticut: "I was happy there, in West Virginia, but I got an itch to see some more world—"

"Connecticut?" asked Walt, amazed.

"That's just where I've ended up. But anyway, I flew out. First over a beautiful horse country, nested round about by white fences—then farms, an' still more farms. Cities, too. But I'm not too partial to cities. There was one *horrenjous* big one, thought—never seen so many buildin's, such smoke—"

"New York!" interrupted Chester Cricket, remembering his summer down there, his adventures and his friends. "Oh, isn't it wonderful."

"Maybe *you* think so, friend cricket—but it scared the tail feathers off of me! Couldn't wait to get past."

"But, Mr. Mockingbird—" began Walter.

"Ashley," said Ashley. "Otherwise I'll be obliged to call you Mr. Snake, friend Walt. Fact is, in West Virginia I'm most respectful of snakes. We keep our distance, though."

"*Ashley*, then—why did you land here? In a meadow that's surrounded by a little town that wants to grow up and be a city."

"Just this is the reason. I saw a little bitty thread of smoke. An' follered it. Then, nearer, this cabin hove into view. It all just reminded me of our people back home. You're very like to see a cabin, in one of the hollers. And there was that mountain, too." Ashley swept his wing toward the west, where Avon Mountain loomed. Deep rays of the sun made the trees on the summit stand out like living men. "You're like to see a mountain like that—"

"Avon Mountain."

"—back home. And our people do love to watch the sun set over somethin' that grand. A mountain like that provides us with protected places. Mountains shelter us. So what with the mountain an' this ramshackle shack—I thought I'd better settle here. The old man, too—"

"Mr. Budd."

"He *has* been so hospitable! Pumpkin seeds—corn. An' *so* complimentary!—about mah little ordinary country songs."

"They're not so—"

But Ashley was too shy for compliments. He rushed right on, through Chester's praise. "Also, he evicted that grumbly big blue jay, so's I could sit on his strong iron bird. Jays are always so ready to take offense."

"Being hit in the head with a squash doesn't help their temper, either," said Simon.

"But anyway," Ashley went on, "I thought I'd stay a day or two. Before startin' back."

"Oh, no!" exclaimed Chester.

"Don't you dare!" threatened Walt, with no venom in his voice.

"Please don't go," mumbled Dubber. "You mean so much to Mr. Budd." He lowered his eyes, and crossed his forepaws, and let his head hang down on them. The hound in him had come out. "And you mean—to me, too."

"Well—well—we'll see." Ashley cleared his throat with another song. "An' I'm gettin' homesick for Hank an' Eller. Also, I've seen the world, now. As much as I need."

"Are Hank and Ella human beings?" asked Chester.

"As human as a human can get!"

"Do they own you?"

Ashley laughed. His mirth, too, was a melody. "No one owns a mockin'bird. But I love them. An' they love me. Want to hear how we three met up? An' their kids?"

"Yes!"—"Yes!"—"Oh, yes!" Snake, cricket, dog, turtle—they made up a curious audience, for a mockingbird. But they all had to hear.

" 'Bout two years ago I was still pretty young, an' still lookin' for mah own tree. Well, one Sunday, flyin' over a holler I hadn't inspected before, I seen this formidable oak. It was growin' real proud right in front of a house that looked like four cabins nailed together, with a porch out front. An' there was a hammock strung up on the porch, huge hammock strung from the two

house beams. On the hammock was dozin' this big ol'
coal miner. I knew, 'cause try as they do a miner can't
get all the black out from under his nails. This one
wasn't ol', though—but, boy, was he big!—just vergin'
thirty, I guess. An' tired, I could see that, from minin'
the coal all week. Clean crispy clothes, though, since
it was Sunday, with a crease in his shirt you could cut
cake with. I started to sing—that's the way a mockin'-
bird tries out a tree—an' this bruiser woke up. He
listened a minute, then went into the house and came
back out with a hunk of corn bread. He crumpled it up
an' held out his hand. I knew what he wanted, but I
was scared. Six six at least—an' almost as big as the
oak! Could've crumpled me, too, with his little finger,
along with corn cake in the palm of his hand. We've
got a few bad ones in West Virginia, too. But he did
look so tired—and wistful in his eyes. I thought—I'll
risk it! What's one mockin'bird more or less? So I
flew down an' lighted on the giant's thumb. So many
calluses on that thumb I hardly could get a grip. Giant
didn't budge a notch, however, an' out of the corner of
mah eye I could see him smilin'. So I munched up the
corn crumbs in that big hard hand. Delicious! But even
more fulfillin' was the smile on that coal miner's face."

Ashley hesitated—then sang a song that the others
hadn't heard before.

"When I had a full tummy, I gave him a song—
right there on his thumb. Big fella shivered, like a tree

in a storm. But I don't think he shivered from worry or fear. I would have given a second song, too—except, right then, his six kids came screamin', tearin', out of the house. They'd heard me singin', an' they scared me half to death, they did. I dashed up to mah oak. But I'm here to tell y'all"—Ashley laughed, like a small water-fall—"their big ol' Daddy chewed them kids out some-thin' wonderful, for frightenin' me that way. They're good kids, though: Richard, Wally, Hank junior, and Tom, and Sally and Sue are the girls. They hushed up Sunday-nice that day. Then Eller came out, when she'd finished the dishes, an' said, 'Hank, what's wrong?' That's Mommy an' Daddy's names—Hank and Eller. 'Nothin',' said Hank. 'Just sit still an' listen.' An' that they both did. Kids, too. Mah Eller has pale blue eyes, kind of watery and exhausted—I would be too, with six kids an' no help!—but beautiful yellow hair. Hank's a redhead with dark brown eyes, like a deer I once met in a holler."

The mockingbird began to unfold his song again. Then he cut it off, to finish his story. "I sang to them all afternoon. First sad—then getting happier—with a perk-up tune at the end. I knew that day that the big oak tree would be mah tree—an' Hank an' Eller, kids too, were going to be mah family."

Ashley finished his song. With no word spoken, the other animals knew that this was the music he'd sung on a Sunday afternoon for the human beings he'd made his own.

He glanced off, embarrassed at having said so much. "I guess they'd never have listened to me if they could've afforded a radio."

"*I* think they would!" said Walter Water Snake seriously. "I sure would have."

"Well—maybe." Ashley glanced at the weather vane. "Big ol' iron birds can't sing to our people. But sometimes I think *I* can!" Then he laughed, and added philosophically, "The good Lord willin'—an' the creek don't rise."

"What's that?" croaked Simon, who'd been listening attentively. Even his shell seemed to pay attention.

"It's just a sayin'," Ashley explained. "Our people say it a lot, back home. Spring especially, a family can get washed out. Not even get across a holler to holler for neighbors to come and help."

Simon coughed out the best laugh he'd had in ten years. "I'm glad you're here, youngster—" For Simon Turtle anyone under thirty-five was a youngster. "You can help."

"I can help with what?"

"With what's asleep in that cabin right now," said Chester. "I'll explain—"

Very often the fun of an explanation depends on how many participate: in this case a cricket, a turtle, a water snake, and a brown-and-white dog with a stomach that hung like a hammock.

"An' I thought we had troubles in mah beautiful blue-ridged mountains!"

46

Ashley

The explanations might well have turned into a shouting match, if not a downright brawl. But before the voices could overlap, the problem himself appeared. The cabin door swung wide, and Mr. Budd emerged. His stomach, like Dubber's, was lordly. And when he stood straight up, on the steps made of good flat stones that he'd built to his house, full beard, with his thumbs hitched into his belt, he did appear lordly. The Old Meadow opened before him like the property of a diminished king. He'd been woken up by the sound of a turtle's laughter—a rasp that he'd never heard before. He liked it, the same way he liked a new flower he'd never yet seen in the meadow grass.

He scratched his beard, white streaked with gray, put two fingers in his mouth, and whistled. "Where are you, my friend?"

"That's me!" whispered Dubber proudly.

He bounded off, barking joyously, through the vegetable patch and was just about to lick Mr. Budd's hand when the old man pushed his head away. "Not you, Dub. You'll scare him. Where is my songbird, anyway?"

Dubber scootched down and hid inside himself.

"Come on now, my singer," called Mr. Budd, with a plea in his voice both sad and sweet. "Don't leave me alone."

"Mm-*mm!*" muttered Ashley, and shook his head. There was no music in his great throat now. "Old man's not alone. Dubber's dyin' to keep him company.

47

An' I *don't* like to see a good dog's feelin's get hurt."

"Me, neither," said Walt, who was wavering up, to get a better view. There lay Dubber, downhearted among the tomato vines. "Not even a dumb mutt like—"

"Hush up now, snake!" the mockingbird ordered. "There's love in that mutt. Somewhere."

The mutt swallowed his humiliation, which tasted worse than an uncooked turnip, and made his way through the beans. When he could see Ashley, he jerked his head toward the cabin roof, and his sad eyes begged. His droopy ears seemed to plead as well. He lay flat, to listen.

"Dog wants me to go," said Ashley, "an' sing. The ol' man likes a song at sundown. But this one's for Dubber. Y'all wait here."

"We all will," said Walt. When Ashley had leaped through the air to the weather vane, he quietly asked Chester Cricket, "Do you understand that mocking-bird?"

"No. I don't need to understand."

Ashley perched on the iron bird's neck and began a sunset song. It was all about colors. They were woven together, in the mockingbird's voice. Blue sky, still shining in the bright sunlight—but orange and red were preparing themselves in the west, behind Avon Mountain—and over all, a burning gold.

The animals clustered on the bank lost themselves

in Ashley's song. So did Mr. Budd. He sat on his three-legged stool, which was always placed on the lowest stone step, as if it were a throne and he were an unacknowledged lord being welcomed home by night at last.

Dubber, who was still scootched in the beans, hardly dared to breathe. He'd rather have died than interrupt his master's bliss.

The song wasn't finished, but "Trouble!" Chester Cricket said. "Ashley said we had troubles. He only meant the human worries. Us animals are just as bad. Look—"

Across Pasture Land a tight hard knot made of blue-and-white wings, like a spiteful small cloud in the air, was flying furiously toward the cabin of Abner Budd—and toward Ashley Mockingbird.

FOUR

J. J. Jay

"Oh, I wish he'd waited till the song was over!" Simon's shell creaked as he shook his head.

"When did J.J. wait for anything?" hissed Walter Water Snake, and he sounded for once as if he was angry and dangerous.

"Okay!" J.J. landed, an iron grip on an iron wing. "We're going to have this out! Right now!"

"What's that, Mr. Jay?" Ashley broke off his song and moved away respectfully. "Have what out? There's lots of room—"

"Who owns this weather vane!" squawked J.J. "It's been my perch for months!"

"Then welcome to it! But that ol' man down there— I just thought that he wanted a change—*watch out!*"

Ashley pushed J.J. to one side, just in time for the blue jay to dodge an unripe tomato. "He's woke up."

"Don't you shove me—!"

"But that tamater—"

"And don't apologize!"

"Well, I would," said the baffled mockingbird. "If I had somethin' to apologize for. Here comes another—!"

"He'll never hit me!" squawked J.J., and ducked. "This time of day I thought he'd stay asleep. No matter. In sunset, an old man's eyes are no good. He's missed me with junk from his garden before. *Aw-haw!* That stupid vegetable garden!" The blue jay preened himself—smoothed out his feathers—as if proving a bird's superiority. After all, what were vegetables compared to the speed hidden in a blue jay's wings.

"Oh, gee," whispered Dubber to Chester, "I hope Mr. Budd doesn't throw them all. The tomatoes were coming so good this year."

"He won't," said Chester. "He'll start to feel how full they are. Then start on the corn, most likely. The ears are still only half grown, and green."

"Is nothing safe?"

"Shh! Ashley and J.J. are talking."

The animals, of course, could understand bird talk. To Mr. Budd it just sounded like two feathered souls, on his weather vane, who were having a vigorous conversation.

"You drove me off my perch!"

"*I* didn't! That man—"

"He's a dopey old man! I'd point into the wind all day myself, if he'd just let me sit here."

"I think that's right fine—"

"Just wait'll you get bean-balled by a squash."

J. J. Jay

"Seems we've moved on to another course. Never did like squash. Tomatoes, now—but J.J., seriously—I didn't want—"

"And how do you know my name?"

"Mah new friends down there—"

"Oh, them!" J.J. shot a contemptuous look at the animals looking up at him. On purpose he rasped his ugliest laugh. "They just common field folk!"

Down below, in the hedge, Chester Cricket was wondering just whom the blue jay was ridiculing, with his raucous squawk: the field folk, Ashley Mockingbird—or was he, somehow, grating angrily on himself? Everybody and himself too? Most likely.

"They seem right nice to me," said Ashley. Unconsciously, he kept his voice monotonous. Somewhere in his head a thought said: Ashley, it's *your* voice is the problem. "I'm sorry about that squash, Mr. Jay. I wouldn't like it a bit myself. An' if this is your perch—"

"Don't fly away!" J.J. tried to demand. Beneath the order, the mockingbird heard a hidden plea. A mockingbird's ears are delicate. Or else how could they sing back the world? "You stay right there!"

"Watch out now! Somethin' orange approachin'!"

A badly aimed carrot flew by.

"I told you! The old fool's sight is going," scoffed J.J. "His mind, too. He might have hit you."

"Birds' eyes go, too," said Ashley. "When we get of an age. I even knew an owl—"

The Old Meadow

"I'm not interested in your broken-down friends!" said J.J. "I've been sitting up here, on this perch, for months. And I serve a purpose, too! Why I—I'm downright useful! Apart from helping this iron thing point into the wind—and sometimes it *needs* help, too, it's rusty—I often make sounds." J.J. couldn't quite bring himself to say "squawk." "When danger approaches. Like a thunderstorm. We had one last week. I—shouted and shouted. Did anyone care? Did any field creep *appreciate* me! Not a one. Not even that dope Donald Dragonfly! And he could be knocked cold by one hardy raindrop."

"Seems to me you do perform a—"

"And *you!* You just sing!"

"That's all I do," Ashley had to admit. "Watch out!"

J.J. ducked—needlessly. The splattering he and Ashley got was as weak as rain, and not even a thunderstorm. A silly green shower of lima beans fell all around them on the roof. "It's getting twilight. He can't stay awake in the dark."

J.J. was right. Because after that handful of lima beans Mr. Budd decided on one more squash: he'd had so much success before. But this one was big and heavy —and fell far short of the weather vane. Throwing great big vegetables in the ripe afternoon was one thing, but twilight, lovely as it was, seemed to bring on an old man's arthritis. Mr. Budd was lame, and tired, too. He sat on his stool, and dozed again.

J. J. Jay

Trees, too, get tired—flowers, grass. The leaves begin
to show it first. They start to droop. The Old Meadow
seemed to exhale a breath as the golden light over
Avon Mountain was slowly overcome by a dark blue
radiance, and then a purple that deepened into the
star-struck night.

The animals in the Old Meadow never saw the sun
set on the horizon. Avon Mountain, a shape of shadow
in the west, always hid it. Chester Cricket often spent
time by himself in wondering what kind of life lived
on Avon Mountain, and how the sunset looked from
there.

Mr. Budd began to snore.

"J.J.," whispered Ashley, "would y'all mind if I
sang Mr. Budd a lullaby? It works real good for the
youngest kids of a couple I know in West Virginia.
Hank Junior had the measles once—forgot to get his
shots—an' this tune just sent him right off to sleep,
even when he was at his sickliest."

"Oh, go ahead!" said J.J., sulking. "A stupid song
for a stupid old man."

Ashley Mockingbird began. He tried not to make
his melody sad, since he'd learned of Mr. Budd's
troubles, but not silly and cheery either, like a shower
of unripe notes. The song did its job. Sunk deep in his
sleep, Mr. Budd grumbled something down into his
beard. Somewhere, in his fear, he knew he might fall
off his stool—tumble into the yard. That warning

roused him, though his eyes were still closed, and like a blind man he went into the cabin. And there, on his mattress, he did fall asleep.

"All right! The old geezer's—"

"*Shh!*" Ashley tried to warn. "The first few minutes are very important. They set the dreams."

"That's just superstition!"

"Maybe so—but it works."

J.J. sulked and fidgeted, while Ashley slowly unrolled his song. It was a melody that said farewell to the day that was done. In his cabin, and deep inside his soul, Mr. Budd heard and sighed. It was one more day that he'd been alone, but hadn't minded. The Old Meadow—its life—had been enough. In his heart, without knowing it, Mr. Budd was keeping count of those days.

"Okay!" J. J. Bluejay burst out. "Mr. Mockingbird —now what's so special about you? That everyone makes such a fuss?"

"Nothin'," Ashley said.

"Then why does Mr. Budd—and those varmints down there—think you're such a prize?"

"Can't imagine." Ashley shifted to a firmer perch. He dreaded something he felt was coming, and thought that he'd better hold on. "I don't have near the beauty of your feathers, J.J. Those blues and whites—and the wonder spread of those wide fine wings."

"You have that voice!"

J. J. Jay

There it was, out loud. Now Ashley understood completely. He looked down, through the deepening evening, to where his friends were listening, watching, waiting—and fearing—on the bank.

"All critters got their gifts—"

"Yes, but *you* have that voice!" J.J. sounded angry. It made Ashley afraid, as if J.J. bore him a personal grudge.

"An' you have your voice, too. A voice which is right for you, J.J."

"I don't like this," Chester Cricket whispered to Simon, down on the bank. "It's *awful* not to like yourself! J.J. is furious! Something bad's going to happen."

"Let's have a contest." J.J. stamped hard on the iron wing of the bird that was harder, much harder, than he. It hurt his foot, but he wouldn't admit it. "I'll beat you! And with my *voice*."

"If you say so, J.J." Ashley felt a shiver where his feathers fitted into his body—always a bird's most sensitive place. He wished he'd never left West Virginia. Too late, though, he knew. J.J.'s feathers were all fluffed up by his rage, and every one was bristling.

"I've got to do mah worst," the mockingbird reminded himself.

"What's that—!"

"Nothin', J.J. Proceed. If you must."

Chester Cricket had hopped, in a nervous fit, right into the middle of the vegetable patch. He settled beside Dubber Dog, who was equally worried. Walter Water Snake, after a soothing dip in the brook—he always took one before going topside—had slithered after him. And even Simon Turtle had crawled up as far as he could. He barely got as far as the beans.

"I really don't like this," said Chester—to Dubber, Walter, the night; he was talking to himself. "J.J. is furious." His antennae jittered. "It's awful not to like yourself," he murmured again.

"Let's go!" squawked the blue jay. "And I'll go first."

"He's had such a pitiful life," chirped a voice from the dark. "Oh, J.J.—"

Oh, J.J. . . .

After Mr. Budd, J. J. Bluejay was the problem person in the whole Old Meadow.

His real name was Jonah Jeremiah Bluejay. That was problem enough. He hated his name, as he hated a lot of everything. His father, George Jay, had been killed by a boy with a BB gun who thought it was fun to shoot at birds. To do the boy credit—his name was Bill Furnivall—he cried a lot when he realized that he'd hit George in the head, where birds can be hurt most easily. As he saw the blue jay drop from the branch he'd been sitting on, he suddenly knew what he'd done and threw his BB gun into the brook. It lies there still, rusted and ugly, and the fish avoid it. So does Walter, and so does Mr. Budd.

Alma Bluejay, Jonah Jeremiah's mother, became a

J. J. Jay

recluse, and wouldn't leave the nest. But J.J. left. And after finding his perch in a beech, the first thing he did, to begin a new life, was change his name. Jonah and Jeremiah sounded awful—like two black grackles. So the young blue jay just picked his initials—J.J. J. J. Bluejay—now there was a name! It sounded like an important person. And he'd whack any bird with his wing who nicknamed him Joe or Jerry or Jer-Jer or anything but J.J. The sparrows insisted on calling him Jerry. They were sociable and silly, and well-meaning too, for all their nonstop chattering. But J.J. whacked the sparrows as well. He was one of the biggest birds in the meadow, and a wingwhack from him could knock a sparrow into tomorrow.

So J. J. Jay it was. The blue jay repeated his name to himself: it sounded—well, like a bird of plumage.

There was nothing, however, that could make J.J. a bird of voice. Blue jays are born with a squawk! That's simply the sound blue jays make. They make another noise, too—a kind of "Doodly-oo," up-and-down sound—but J.J. had never mastered those notes. It may have been that his daddy, George, was never there to teach him, but J.J. was trapped in his squawk. And he hated it. Despite his blue-and-white wings, as lovely as anything in the Old Meadow, and despite the grace with which he alighted on any bough—J. J. Bluejay was mad at himself. That ugly squawk: he could never forgive himself for it.

But also he never could stop attempting to sound

59

as beautiful as his plumage. He'd go way off and find some corner of the Old Meadow that only the insects and wildflowers remembered, and there he'd practice, day after day, all alone with the trees and the wind and the bugs. He was sure that he was improving. And, indeed, he did learn to squawk somewhat softer.

"I'm first!" J.J. demanded again.

"I'm willin'," said Ashley Mockingbird.

J.J. fluffed his wings, which still glimmered in the lingering twilight, as if his feathers might help his voice. Then, since he'd decided to begin with a fanfare, he let out a shriek that almost left Chester Cricket cross-eyed.

"Oh, boy," whispered Chester, who was leaning on a stringbean to recover, "this contest is going to be something special."

"I'm going underwater," said Walt.

"I'm going into my shell," said Simon.

"Oh no, you're not!" the cricket squeaked. He couldn't roar, but he did his best. "You're both going to stay right where you are. We've all got to see this through together. My antennae are telling me that there's more at stake here than a couple of birds on a weather vane."

"What's at stake?" Walter wanted to know.

But Chester didn't have a chance to answer.

"Mah turn?" asked Ashley politely.

"*Yes!*" J.J.'s voice was challenging, hard.

Ashley worked his mouth a bit, to get moisture into

his throat. Then, when he was ready, he aimed for the high note that J.J. had tried to hit, and struck it dead center. The tone swelled over Mr. Budd's cabin, just like the light of the filling moon that was rising in the south.

Ashley Mockingbird seemed to like that note. He held it—and held it—then dipped to a note just below it and sang them together, one after the other, very fast.

"That's a trill," sighed Chester. He leaned on the stringbean now in bliss. "The most beautiful I've ever heard."

"Okay! okay!" On the weather vane, J.J. admitted that he had lost that round.

"Y'all may have had somethin' in your throat—"

"Just listen to *this!*"

J.J. croaked a melody—every note of which would have put out a star. They were just appearing.

"How's *that?*"

"Mighty fine," lied Ashley. "But how about if you an' me did it like this? Just a little bit less crackly maybe—"

Ashley sang the blue jay's melody. And the stars came out again. It was as if a soothing hand had passed over the face of the whole Old Meadow.

J.J. suddenly thought of Alma, his mother, and how one time—there'd been thunder and lightning—she'd lifted her wing to shield him from the rain.

"You're not playing fair!"

61

The Old Meadow

"I sure am! I'm just singin' what you do—"

"You're *mocking* me!" squawked J.J.

"If I was mockin' you—" Ashley Mockingbird had a peaceful and a loving soul, but he, too, could become infuriated. And most of all when he—of all birds—was accused of being cruel. "J.J., if I was mockin' you, like what mah name suggests, I'd let go this!"

In a peal of sound that amazed the fortunate few who heard it, Ashley summoned up all the birdcalls and the animal noises he'd been gathering in his throat from the time that he'd lived in the Old Meadow, and he wove them out in a tapestry of music. In his song there were the conversations of sparrows, the peeps of finches. There was even the snarl of a nasty cat who'd tried to catch John Robin. There was Robert Rabbit's gulp of joy as he downed a carrot. And also Chester's chirp was there, though he never dreamed that he'd be remembered. All the meadow noises were in one throat—but made musical and beautiful.

And lastly, in this collected music, there was Jonah Jeremiah Bluejay himself. Ashley Mockingbird imitated J.J. He made a squawk—high, funny, and ridiculous. Then, even more mischievous, he turned the squawk into something wonderfully lovely, as if to remind the blue jay of what he had always longed for but never could achieve. But even as he made the sounds that derided his fellow bird, who sat beside him on an iron perch, Ashley knew that he'd made a great mistake.

J. J. Jay

Chester knew it too, below, in the dark. "I *wish* Ashley hadn't squawked like that. J.J. has no sense of humor."

Ashley wasn't afraid, but J.J. showed fear. His head jerked away, and his eyes sought the night. His small heart had been devastated—more by the beauty of Ashley's song than by the mockery.

"J.J., I apologize. It's not like me to do that. I hope."

With one rush of his wings, the blue jay rose from the weather-vane wing. He hovered in the moonlight, loomed dark and strange and threatening.

"One of us has got to get up on that roof!" urged Chester Cricket breathlessly. "To stop them."

"I doubt if I—" began Simon Turtle, about to explain why he personally might have a hard time.

"Someone hurry!" interrupted Chester. "It'll be too—"

Already it was too late.

J.J.'s wings—he began to beat them furiously—created a downdraft that almost knocked Ashley off his perch. The mockingbird clung for his very life to that iron wing. In the hollers of his home he had never met a single soul—not even the rattlesnake, when disturbed—as enraged as J. J. Bluejay. But echoing, like a bad off-key tune in the back of his mind, was the fact that he'd never been so unkind himself.

"I *said* I was sorry—"

"You said! You said—!" J.J. idled in the air. His

claws were extended. They looked like talons, as he toyed with this bird, whose pale feathers shone in the pale moonlight. "I heard what you said. And sang— you creep!"

Abruptly the blue jay made a dive and yanked out a feather from Ashley's head. It seemed to excite him, and satisfy his anger. J.J. began to squawk. But he wasn't just making his natural blue-jay sound now. It was an ugly cry of triumph.

"J.J.—stop!" shouted Chester Cricket.

J.J. didn't even hear. He swooped—then regained altitude—then swooped again, to torment the mocking-bird. "You—you *stranger!* You wimp! You come to my Old Meadow, where I've been unhappy all my life, and you start your charm over everyone—"

"Y'all want me to go away?" asked Ashley. He didn't want to get beaten up, but more important, he knew from the pain in J.J.'s anger that a life was at stake— the blue jay's, not his. He'd just launch off and fly back home. But J.J. could not escape from himself. " 'Cause I will! I'll fly—"

"Oh, don't!" barked Dubber.

But neither bird heard. J.J. was beating Ashley now with all the force of his two wings. And he didn't make a squawk while he did it. He was too much afraid of sounding absurd. Yet mercilessly he took out his spite on his enemy.

"There's still a little light in Mr. Budd's cabin—"

J. J. Jay

"Yes, Chester. It's his candle—almost always lit. He can't go to sleep in the total dark."

"Go wake him, Dubber! *Now!*"

Dubber Dog rushed up to the cabin and began to scratch. That didn't make enough noise. He pounded his head on the door. But that hurt. So Dubber howled: his first howl in years, except for the phony howls he made when Mr. Budd tried to whop him.

This desperate howl worked.

Mr. Budd heaved out of his sleep and mumbled, "What? What's that. I am grateful for the corn, Luke!" Then he was awake. "What's goin' on?" He heard the birds screaming on his roof. "What *is* goin' on?" Like a wounded bear, because of the arthritis, Mr. Budd hauled himself off the mattress and limped outside.

What he saw on the tilted roof of his cabin made Mr. Budd forget his own pain. He'd slanted the roof to let the rain run off. But now, on the roof of the home that he'd built for himself and his dogs and his friends from the meadow, a battle of birds was taking place. The iron weather vane seemed loving in comparison.

Life flexed his rigid old bones. "You stop that, darn blue jay!" He picked up a rock, but then just held it, uselessly, in his hand. In this dim light he might have hit the mockingbird. "Please don't, blue jay! Don't hit him no more!"

J.J. was now pounding methodically—his right wing on Ashley's back. He'd always picked on little birds—

the sparrows—out of his own misery, or else just a nasty streak, but Ashley was quite big. He could have put up a fight. But mockingbirds aren't fighters, and Ashley especially was not. To fight seemed not to be musical.

"Do something, Dubber!" shouted Mr. Budd, in despair.

"*Bow-wow-wow!*" hollered Dubber. It wasn't even dog talk. Neither Chester nor Simon nor Walter could understand a word. It was just plain furious barking.

Above, when a chance occurred—J.J. had to catch his breath, because hitting a person who doesn't resist is very tiring—Ashley tried to fly away. J.J. gulped air and took one more swipe with his wing. He hit the mockingbird on the head and stunned him momentarily. He fell to the roof of Mr. Budd's cabin—and the fall did stun him badly. Unconscious, he started to slide. The slant that Abner had built for rain now poured down a mockingbird.

"Oh, mercy!" On the ground, Mr. Budd was running back and forth. His arthritis was all forgotten. "That bird'll break his neck!"

The moonlight was dim. But enough shone off the tar-paper roof so that Abner could follow the limp shape as it slithered down. He positioned himself— held out cupped hands—and thanked the Lord when a soft feathered weight fell into them. It was so still, though.

66

The Old Meadow

"Oh, don't be dead!" pleaded Abner Budd. "Please don't."

Holding Ashley as gently as a man ever held a bird, he rushed into his cabin. Dubber followed. The door swung shut.

By the brook, in the silvered night, the three friends were silent.

On the iron weathervane J.J. spread his wings—more beautiful than he deserved—and flew off, to his beech.

"*I hate you, J.J.!*" shouted Chester Cricket, after him. It was the first time in this cricket's life that he'd ever used the word "hate."

"Come on, now," wheezed Simon. "We've got to go home now. There's times in the life of an animal—birds, too—when it's best to be cared for by human beings. At least the ones who care for us."

FIVE

A Debate

"I am definitely gonna bite that mutt!"

"Where?" asked Donald Dragonfly, who took an interest in everything.

He'd been out on his morning flight—his "constitutional," he called it—and he had decided to visit Chester. Chester Cricket was his best friend. All the field folk knew that Donald was "tetched"—too much light on those glorious wings of his—but Donald Dragonfly didn't care. Life was full of light and colors, and Chester loved Donald for reflecting them all.

It was good he'd flown up this morning. Walt and Chester were frantic, and Simon was as perturbed as an old turtle can get. It had been two days since the fight between J.J. and Ashley. On Simon's advice, the three friends had stayed away from the cabin. Too much prying might make Abner nervous, he said—especially with the worries he had these days; let the Town Council spy on an old man, but not field folk. But when Donald appeared, like a rainbow whirring through the morning sunlight, everybody agreed that he at least could fly upstream and ask Dubber what in the world was happening. The dragonfly had just flown back.

"Simmer down now, Walt," said Chester. "Donald said that Dubber promised to come down in a while and give us a firsthand report."

"Well, where *is* he?"

"It's that new bird, isn't it, Chister?" asked Donald. "The whole meadow knows about him."

"I know—and the whole meadow's going crazy. I had Beatrice Pheasant and both chipmunks here yesterday, demanding to know what's going on. We're all behaving like a lot of giddy bugs in a tizzy."

"I'm a bug," said Donald. "And so are you, Chister." He pondered a moment. "Do you think I'd like a tizzy? I could try to be in one—"

With Donald—one had to be careful. "I think you are fine just as you are," said the cricket. "Why don't you spread out your wings now, for a while? That's always relaxing."

The tetched dragonfly elevated his four wings gracefully. A palette of colors fell on Simon's Pool.

"At last!" Walter Water Snake was stretching every inch of himself above the bank. "When we didn't want to see him, he showed up like a bellyache, but now that we're starved for news—! Oh, Dubber, you delightful dog!"

"Are you sick, Walter?" Dubber padded, his potbelly swinging under him, to the edge of the pool. "You never thought I was delightful before."

"Enough of the chitchat!" squeaked Chester. "How's Ashley?"

"Oh, he's fine." Dubber settled his hind legs under him, and scratched his right ear. He'd had a flea there for a week, but hadn't been able to shake him out.

"I like it when someone's fine," murmured Donald.

"The details! The details! See these fangs—?"

"Oh, pull 'em back in!" shouted Chester. "And try to hush up while we find out the really important things." He hopped to the bank and sat beside Dubber.

It was near noon on a day that made the whole world —not only Donald Dragonfly—glow like a multicolored jewel, an opal perhaps, whose colors flash suddenly into light.

"The mockingbird *is* all right—?"

"Injured, but yes. He wasn't hurt bad. After Mr. Budd caught him, we both thought he had a broken wing. But it wasn't. Just sprained. A sprained wing is all it was, where Ashley hit the roof so hard."

"When can we see him?" asked Chester.

"That's what I came to ask you. Can y'all come upstream right now? Abner's nappin'. He feels safe enough about Ashley now to take his noon snooze."

"I all can't," said Donald. "I take my noon snooze on my twig, and I all can't change."

"Oh, boy!" said Chester. " 'I all'—'y'all'—this

meadow may never recover from one harmless mockingbird."

"And Ashley wants to talk to you, Chester. He says
we have real problems here."

That peeved Chester a little: that he'd have to hear
that piece of news from a stranger. But it also made him
want to laugh. "We don't need a golden-throated singer
to fly out of the South to tell us this." Chester suspected
that everyone's problems were obvious—especially the
ones they tried to hide.

"Anyway, Ashley says come now! Mr. Budd's enough
certain that the bird's on the mend so he's willin' to
take his afternoon nap. So this is a good time for us to
talk. The good Lord willin' —an' the creek don't rise."

"Oh, boy!" said Chester. "One mockingbird."

"Let's go!" said Walter.

"You tell me about it later," said Simon. "I think
I'll just stay here. I find that some news is more exciting
when you hear about it afterwards than when it takes
place right before your eyes." Also, the sun felt like a
kind hand whose fingers were strumming, but very
gently, all over his shell. "Make certain you tell me
everything now." He yawned, as he fell asleep.

"And tell me, too—if I should remember to ask,"
said Donald Dragonfly. He flew home, to his twig over-
hanging the brook. He could always remember that
flight.

Ashley was perched on Luke's stool in front of the

A Debate

cabin, enjoying the sun in his own way, like Simon in his. "Hah, y'all!" he caroled to everyone.

"Mr. Budd still asleep?" whispered Dubber in a baritone rumble that could wake up a rock.

"Asleep an' snorin'. We was up all last night again. He kept askin' me if I could sleep—I kept twitterin' yes—then he'd ask me again ten minutes later—an' we went on like that till dawn."

"You *look* all right," Chester Cricket worried. "And I promise I'll only ask this once: *are* you?"

"This wing here"—Ashley tried to straighten his right wing out, and barely could—"it's mighty sore. That J.J. packs a wallop—"

"He better not come within striking distance!"

"Now, Walt, cool off. Topple back there into the creek. In many ways I had it comin'—an' in other ways, I'm glad it happened. I was showin' off. An' it's all right to show off, but only in front of the folks who want you to show. Like Hank an' Eller. They want me to do my darndest, hidden up in the leaves of mah oak. But here—I wasn't just showin' off, I was showin' J.J. up." Ashley shook his head and warbled a tune of confusion. "I've learned a lot in these few days."

His here-and-there melody straightened out. "There's a lot I've learned. One thing: your human bein's up here aren't an itty-bit like our people. Our people back home, I mean. Why, no one back in West Virginia would heave a man out of his cabin."

"You know the fix we're in," said Chester.

"I think I do. But since that first day, when you explained—betwixt Dubber here an' the ramblin's of Mr. Budd, when he nodded off despite himself—an' sometimes when he just had to talk, an' I was there, bein' tended to in his hands—I got the whole picture. It's pretty ugly." He sang his uncertain song again. "Especially since those guys with the ties have been comin' around again."

Ashley whistled a question. "Y'all short of land up here?"

"It isn't that," Chester said. "I mean—yes, we are. In this part of Connecticut. But the Old Meadow is something special."

"I was raised to believe all the earth was special," said Ashley Mockingbird. "You better had try to tell me more."

Chester flicked his antennae. It helped to fix his thoughts. He told Ashley how the Old Meadow had been made a special place. And he tried to explain the Truce, too: "When the meadow got saved from development—from parking lots and gas stations—we animals got together and resolved that since we were saved we wouldn't attack one another, and not eat each other, unless dangerously provoked."

"And J.J. broke the Truce!" hissed Walter. "He hit you without your hurting him first."

"I 'preciate your kind words," said Ashley, "but maybe I hurt him in ways you don't know."

"No excuse! *I've* got the right to bite him now!"

74

A Debate

"You leave that blue jay to me," said the mocking-bird sternly.

"Then you *are* still going to stay?" muttered Dubber. "Despite J.J."

"Well, I reckon I'll have to. For a while at least. Can't leave Mr. Budd to his pitiful self, under threat of foreclosure—not after the way the good man's taken care of me. In the middle of his own trouble, too. An' J.J."—Ashley looked at the weather vane—"we've got somethin' between us that has to be settled."

A silence took over. And stayed. And stayed. Clouds had covered the meadow. The sky now shone like a cloudy pearl. A layer of dull light hovered over the world. But a mild brightness shone through. This strange misty silence was only interrupted by snores.

"So what're we going to do?" said Chester.

Walter lashed his tail, distractedly, every which way. It's what snakes do when they're all confused. Walter fortunately missed his own head by an inch. When a snake hits himself with himself, that's a sign of real confusion. And also it can become a bad habit.

"How'd y'all decide on this Truce?"

"We got together—all of us—and had a debate—and decided on what we'd do."

"Then that's what you've got to do now," Ashley jumped from the stool to the stones in front of Mr. Budd's first step. A patch of sunlight lingered there. "Get together. Decide. Did you vote on the Truce?"

"Yes, we did," said Chester.

"Then now y'all have to vote on how y'all will help Mr. Budd. Or let him sink."

"The trouble is," said Walter Water Snake, "not all the field folk will want to help. We've got some proud ones here who think Mr. Budd is just a human left-over."

77

The Old Meadow

"Ashley"—Dubber Dog crept forward on his legs, flat down on the earth, the way a dog does when he wants a favor—"will you talk to everyone? You can persuade. You can *sing—!*"

"Oh, I'll sing an' I'll talk"—Ashley tested his wing —"an' I'll fly, too. The good Lord willin' an' the creek don't rise."

The debate about Mr. Budd turned out to be the loudest, longest, and angriest gathering of animals ever held in the Old Meadow. That time when everyone decided to establish the Truce was an afternoon's nap in comparison. The Truce debate had been held beside Simon's Pool. And Henry Chipmunk got so excited he fell in the brook. No one wanted that to happen again —and least of all Henry, who only got fished out because Mr. Budd was walking around and heard this squeaky spluttering.

Mr. Budd's debate was held in Pasture Land, which was dry: an expanse of turf where the cows, in old times which no one remembered, had been put to browse. Also, there were tuffets around. It bordered on Beatrice Pheasant's home, Tuffet Towers, and anyone who wanted to talk could mount a tuffet and make himself heard.

And many did make themselves loudly heard during the Mr. Budd debate. The subject, of course, was Abner. That had been announced by animal, bird, and insect, too, for two days. The time—ripe morning. Eleven o'clock as human beings measured time. The big gold feeling, as field folk measured it. In an hour the sun would be right at the summit of heaven. There'd be no shadows at all. That was a scary, shivery moment—no shadows!—for all things that lived. Everybody asked himself: Am I here?

Chester opened the proceedings, from the top of a modest tuffet: "The question, Field Folk, is—*do* we try to help Mr. Budd?"

Beatrice Pheasant, as usual, was the first to speak. She mounted a tuffet, took a quick look around at her beautiful feathers, and said, "I, for one, am rather glad that the matter of Mr. Budd—"

"Hooray for him!" shouted Henry Chipmunk. "I'd be drowned without him."

"Well, he chased me right into the brook!" said Bill Squirrel. "I was only looking for acorns, too, underneath his porch—"

"He never chased *me!*" interrupted Robert Rabbit. "Just as long as I stay in my half of the carrot-and-lettuce patch, he's as nice as grass. He even likes to watch me munch out, through that slippery window of his."

"He tried to drown me," remembered Paul Mole. "Poured water down my front door."

"You were ruining the little lawn the old man has made," said Robert. "If you'd struck a bargain, to

live under only half—like me in his garden—he'd
probably—"

"Oh, he's not *nice!*" fussed Beatrice. "He's old, and
sometimes—he doesn't wash!"

"The brook's cold sometimes!" said Dubber. "I'd
like to see *you*—"

Donald Dragonfly tried to get in a buzz, but no one
paid any attention. Donald wasn't insulted: he'd
already forgotten what he wanted to say.

"Please! Please!" chirped Chester. "We'll never get
anywhere, if everyone talks at once."

Somewhere in his antennae, however, Chester
Cricket knew that a lot of the fun of a great debate
was in interrupting. He felt a twitch to shout himself.
But he held himself steady and did his duty, as chair-
cricket of this meeting.

"I'd like to hear from Ashley Mockingbird," said
Chester, very businesslike. "Y'all—I mean, everybody
knows that Ashley is our guest here this summer, and
he's gotten to be Mr. Budd's best friend."

"His best?" Dubber lifted his long ears up and
blinked his soulful brown eyes.

"*One* of his best," Chester's voice retreated. "I think
Ashley might enlighten us as to—"

"I think I might enlighten you, too! Aw! Haw!"

J. J. Jay, on his skillful wings, rode down through
the air and alighted gracefully beside Chester on the
Speaker's Tuffet. He'd been sulking, brooding, in his

80

beech for these two days—part from anger, and part humiliation, and part—who knows what? Nerves, not remorse.

Ashley Mockingbird was standing just below Chester. His wing was still sore, and he'd barely been able to limp through the air down to Pasture Land. There was a very difficult minute between J.J. and Ashley: that moment between confused guys who've had a fight and can't yet reach each other again. Eyes avoided eyes.

As soon as Walter saw J.J. glide down, he raced like black lightning straight up to the tuffet. "I mean this, J.J.!—my teeth have been a joke up till now—but I'll take off your legs if you lay one feather on Ashley!"

"Oh, don't worry!" J.J. scoffed. "I won't beat up on this wimp again."

"Take that back—!"

"Forget it, Walt." Ashley patted the snake on the back of his head. That's something that doesn't happen often. Even under the binding spell of the Truce. A snake and a bird. All the animals looked up in awe at this gesture of friendship. "I got the respect of the people I like."

"Aw, *haw!*" laughed J.J. "You field fools can just stop your talkin'! You can't save the old geezer, anyway. I happened to be near the cabin this morning— had to get off my beech and stretch my wings—and more of those town inspectors came down. Mr. B. was asleep—old geezers sleep more and more as they age. And our musical star from the South was asleep too, I would guess. I didn't hear any soulful tunes emanating from that ramshackle shack. Aw! haw!" J.J. taunted, and fluffed up his feathers.

"I did take a nap. The wing heals in sleep."

"The neckties from the Town Council agreed that that 'unsightly' cabin—"

"There's that *word* again!" groaned Dubber.

Chester Cricket groaned, too. And in his mind he agreed. Words were powerful. If someone would just call Mr. Budd's dilapidated cabin "picturesque" or "quaint," there might not be all this worry all over.

"They also agreed," went on J.J., "to vote on the matter this week."

"Y'all do a lot of votin' up here," said Ashley.

"This *is* New England," Simon Turtle explained. "Town meetings—you know—all that."

"But then we still have time!" exclaimed Chester. "A week."

"Time for *what?*" the blue jay demanded.

"Why, to help Mr. Budd."

"Oh, help," squawked J.J. "And just how do you know that all of us field folk want to help? He's *old*, Mr. Budd is—and getting foolish."

"I like old folks!" shouted Henry Chipmunk. "They're nice."

"Good for you," wheezed Simon, who'd had his shell quite a while himself.

A Debate

"Let's everybody vote," said Ashley. "Since that's what y'all seem to like the most."

"I propose a motion," said J.J., "that we let the old fool get thrown out. They'll make a nice park space where that rickety shanty is now. And also, that ugly weather vane—which he throws vegetables at, when I sit there—well, it'll be *gone!* For good!"

"Hold on," Ashley said. "Now I know I'm a stranger, but what would your Ol' Meadow be without Mr. Budd?" Ashley sang a tune with a questions hidden in its notes. "You meadow folk—what would y'all be without a single human bein'? A different kind of soul in your world."

"We'd be better off!" squawked J.J.

A commotion of animal sounds broke out. Ashley Mockingbird had meant to say and sing more of his thought, but he couldn't be heard.

To silence the din, the oldest voice in the meadow spoke out: "And I propose"—Simon Turtle couldn't quite make the climb to the tuffet—"that we field folk help Mr. Budd."

Both motions were seconded, thirded, and fourthed, and were thoroughly confused in a storm of voices that demanded that they be heard.

But voting began, somehow.

The large animals were no problem: they just shouted "Yes!" or "No!"—and some added that everyone else was a nitwit. Beatrice Pheasant and her obedient husband, of course, voted no. Robert Rabbit voted yes twice, but Chester saw him, when he sneaked around, and ruled out the second yes. Paul Mole didn't vote at all. He abstained. In a private debate, he was thinking about half a lawn. After all, it might be better than none.

The insects were difficult. Apart from the job of collecting votes from so many of them, some insects can't decide on a thing. They dither and fidget— oftentimes in the air. Donald Dragonfly took an hour to make up his mind himself. He finally voted yes, but mostly because he didn't know what no meant. Despite his blurred mind, however, which was often just as kaleidoscopic as the light on his wings, Donald organized a hive of bees. They lived in the ruins of Chester's old home, that broken-down stump. He kept saying, "Hey, you guys—you've got enough honey. We need your help." Bees are reasonable people, and at last they agreed to collect the insect vote. It was, they all communicated to one another, the only way to get rid of Donald.

After the bees reported in, the problem and the debate were over. So everyone thought. The animals voted to help Mr. Budd.

"Haw! haw!" That's great!" cawed J.J. His harsh cry didn't sound one little bit defeated. "Now tell me, you sweet field people—*awk!*" Even J.J. had to choke on the mean small pleasure he felt. It lodged in his throat and made his voice even uglier. "Just *how* are you going to help the old bum?"

84

A Debate

"My Mr. Budd's no bum!" woofed Dubber.

"When they come with pickaxes at his house—just *how*—just *what* are you going to do?"

With the furious grace of someone who had lost an election but made a point, J.J. flew away.

Those two questions—how? what?—like invisible hummingbirds' wings beat furiously in the thickening light of afternoon, even after the blue jay had gone.

Chester suddenly realized, "We don't *know* how—"

"Tchoor we do! At least"—Walter's head drifted vaguely, like a little balloon at the end of a string—"we'll think of something. Everybody go home and think!"

Everybody went home and thought, all right. But as usual, this time of day, most field folk thought about dinner and sleep.

Not Ashley and Chester, however. The mockingbird thought it best not to risk another flight with that wing, so he and the cricket hopped, side by side, to the cabin. They'd both been wanting to know each other—and more than just as respectful friends. This seemed a good time to hop the last step, or sing the last note of openness.

"I surely am learnin' a lot—up here in Connecticut," said Ashley.

"So am I," said Chester. "And a lot of what I'm learning I don't like."

"Don't take on, now. Things have a way of working out."

The Old Meadow

"Maybe in West Virginia," said Chester. "The good Lord willin'—an' the creek don't rise."

Now solid friends, the two of them laughed. Ashley clapped the cricket on the back with the wing that wasn't sore, and Chester pretended to give a hurt chirp.

"I think I'll sing Abner a special sundown song," said Ashley. "It's Eller's favorite. I think she likes it because it reminds her of the quilt she's stitchin'. Her grandmama started it—then Eller's ma—an' then her, too. It's a beautiful thing that she's tryin' to do between housecleanin' an' changin' diapers. I hope to weave in mah colors, too. Want to listen?"

"The Hawk couldn't scare me away! Can you make it to the weather vane?"

"I think I'll settle for that little ol' stool."

Ashley Mockingbird crutched up through the sunset, and landed, gladly, on Mr. Budd's stool. He began his song. It was indeed a quilt of memory and new threads, fine filaments of music that Ashley seemed to spin from his throat.

Chester cocooned himself in the beauty.

Then—something got his attention.

He chirped—urgently. And a cricket like Chester doesn't chirp at sunset. Chester loved the night, which was punctured by stars. He chirped three more times. Ashley knew that the cricket was warning him. He dropped down from the stool, still favoring that wing, and asked, "Cricket friend, don't you like mah ol'-fashioned song?"

86

A Debate

"I love it. But look over there."

On the other side of the brook, three people were watching. And listening.

"I know who the kid is," said Chester. "His name is Alvin, and he likes to tease us animals. I don't know who the big guys are."

"They do look pretty foolish to me," said Ashley. "Those baggy pants—and an *orange* T-shirt—?"

"Foolish can be dangerous." Chester hated to sound like a judge. But he did, quite frequently, and often—despite himself—he was right. "They're—observing you! Will you sing in the house from now on? It's too easy to attract a crowd. I did it myself when I lived in New York."

"What a life!" said Ashley. "I was hopin' mah voice could *help* Mr. Budd—"

"It still may—"

"—an' now I've got to sing indoors!" The mockingbird whistled his anger and disbelief. "Cooped up! Confined!" He trilled a lullaby. "I suppose I'll have to learn to be *cozy!*"

SIX

Fights!

Robert Rabbit liked vegetables almost as much as Abner Budd did.

Robert lived in a very private place. An elm tree, blighted, had fallen down, and its branches, all tangled, got overgrown with vines. There were shady, lovely, secret spaces where a rabbit could relax and feel safe.

Every day, when Robert woke up, the first thing he did was his wake-up shake. Then a rabbit's steady hunger set in. Most often Robert Rabbit said to himself, "Might see how Mr. Budd's doing today."

On the way to inquire after Mr. Budd's health, Robert did his exercises. It helped that there was a flat piece of Pasture Land that he passed where the grass was worn down. No need to try to eat here, he knew, because something much better was up ahead. His exercise he called "getting my running feet." That meant that on the smooth green turf he ran round and round in widening circles until his flying feet felt like wings. Then he knew he was ready for the whole full

Fights!

day, rain or shine. And especially ready for Mr. Budd's garden.

Yesterday, on the morning of the debate, he'd had— what *had* he had? Rabbits scratch their ears like dogs, with their hind legs: *tckktchktchk!*—just like that, much faster than human eyes can see.

He'd had beet greens!

Robert Rabbit arrived at his favorite spot: the exact center of his half of Mr. Budd's garden. Around him glowed all the vegetables. The beet greens—their red hearts were underground. The frilly fronds of carrot tops. And the gangly string beans, too, like awkward boys, were ripening. Robert loved even the vegetables that he didn't eat himself—unless famished. Their colors were so beautiful. The mysterious purple of the royal eggplant. What secrets did its full roundness contain? The sunny yellow of squash, always on vacation. Rich, red tomatoes, fat and satisfied with their full piggy bank. Robert sighed in delight: the glory of vegetables—*everywhere!*

Best of all, his favorite if there had just been a rain— though the human beings didn't think much of it— the ordinary, good green grass. It was especially luscious in the little lawn Mr. Budd had created in front of his home. Robert always saved that for dessert.

He settled in for his morning's breakfast of sheer contentment.

And before he took a bite of bean a cardboard box was all around him.

The Old Meadow

"I've gotcha now!" a mean voice snickered above the darkness where Robert was caught. Of course, his capture could never have happened at all if Robert hadn't been so greedy that he forgot his animal's attention. It's a lesson they all have to learn: be wary at all times—of everything!

"You Alvin, you!" But somebody had been paying attention.

Inside his cabin, Mr. Budd had silently lifted a corner of glassine window to watch Robert nibble his dewy meal. He didn't need to be quiet about it. The rabbit had caught him often enough. But secrecy—the sly lifting and looking—was most of the joy of a man peeking at a rabbit. That long-eared friend. Then, too, he liked to make sure that Robert—but Mr. Budd called him Longears—stayed in his half of the garden.

"You Alvin—I'll whop your bottom!" This attack by a boy on a rabbit had ruined a wonderful game.

The cabin door burst open. Arthritis and age were left inside. Mr. Budd dashed out barefoot. A privet hedge, which he'd planted twenty years ago, had hidden Alvin and his sinister cardboard box from the old man smiling behind his window. Otherwise, Alvin would have been stopped before he reached the lettuce.

Ashley Mockingbird, his wing getting better day by day, flew out of the cabin, too, and made it, like a mountain climber, to the beak of the weather vane.

In his darkness, trapped, Robert Rabbit felt the

cardboard box shake, as Alvin—whoever he was—ran away. Then he got tipped over. Mr. Budd's big feet had run by. Robert dashed to freedom. But he didn't dash too far. He felt free by the end of the last row of beans. And he wanted to watch the ruckus that he knew was about to occur.

"You, Alvin Irvin—you stay right here!"

As if there was anything Alvin could do. A shivering boy of ten was held by the hair in the grasp of a man old enough to be his granddad. Abner Budd had won that race, toward the brook, through the vegetable garden.

"Lemme go!"

"I will not! Why are you persecuting my rabbit?"

"I *felt* like it—you old goat!"

Mr. Budd sat down and with his right leg locked the boy firmly across his left knee.

On the other side of the yard, Dubber winced. He knew what was coming, and he knew how it felt. On the weather vane, Ashley sang a pacifying song, but Mr. Budd was too furious to hear.

His flattened right hand—a silent whop—was lifted in the air. He knew he'd have to force himself to spank this boy, but a good rabbit was a good rabbit, and a bad kid was—

"You're just like my grandma!" Alvin wailed.

"Why am I like your grandma?" The whop was stayed where it was, uplifted. This bad kid was miser-

Fights!

able, in his tie-dyed T-shirt, raggedy short pants, and dirty sneakers. Even his freckles, as he craned his face around, looked like a map of unhappiness.

"She's mean, too. Like you! *All* old folks are mean!"

"How's your grandma mean?"

"She won't let me learn to hang-glide," gleeped Alvin.

"Hang-gliding! Well, I should think not!" The undelivered whop lowered. Abner's hand rested gently on Alvin's back, though his right leg, still strong despite the arthritis, kept him tackled across his knee. "How old are you, Alvin Irvin?" From listening and listening down through the years, Mr. Budd knew the names, first and last, of all the children—and all the adults who had once been children—who roamed through the Old Meadow. But not one of them knew that his first name was Abner.

"I'm 'leven!" said Alvin. "And I'm grown up! I want to hang-glide down from Avon Mountain and fly over everywhere. Especially the meadow. There's a hang-glider takeoff place up there. I know—my dad and my uncle took me."

Abner Budd released the boy. The young fellow didn't move, however. There was no whop anywhere now.

"It would be nice," murmured Abner. The dream of flight, to feel finally at home, in the sky, set his spirit soaring. "If I could do it, I'd follow the course

of the brook first: down from Avon Mountain, then
over the dam at the reservoir—then zigzag through the
meadow—"

"Me, too!" peeped Alvin, whose voice hadn't
changed.

"Then I'd zoom back over Pasture Land, Tuffet
Country, and look at my cabin—from way up high!
Lordy me—that would be strange—to see my home
like a bird." Mr. Budd had a reverie, for a minute.
"And if I ever came down again—which I might not—
and got back, I'd feel as if my place was blessed. Since
it had been seen from someplace up high."

The thought was so new that it made Abner tremble.
But it was the best kind of chill to feel: a shudder before something wonderful.

"But look here, boy"—he stood Alvin up and held
him steady, with two big hands on little thin shoulders
—"even if you and me got the same kind of dreams,
and even if you can't hang-glide yet, that's no reason
for you to capture my rabbit. And not even if you was
to make him a pet." Abner hoped that that was the explanation.

"But I can't reach that bird."

"*What*—!"

"Well, if I can't fly, I want to have a pet who can—"

"In a *cage*?"

"—and who also sings. Like that one on your
weather vane. My dad and my uncle and I have been
listening all this week."

Fights!

"Oh, you boy!"

Alvin Irvin was whirled around, bottom up, and—

Whop!

Only one *whop* was heard in the vegetable garden, but many "*ow's*" resounded through the whole Old Meadow. They bounded loudly off the stone wall and ricocheted among the trees. Alvin was sure that he'd felt more than one *whop!* He hadn't.

"Now you get outa here, you boy!" shouted Abner Budd. "And tell your grandma that if I ever catch you again—puttin' boxes on my rabbit, or even *thinkin'* of catchin' my bird!—well, I'll, I'll kick your little behind so hard that you'll hang-glide all right! But no wings! Get *goin'*!"

It was later on that day, when the sun had just begun to slide down the round afternoon, that the strangest sight ever seen—so far—in the history of the Old Meadow appeared.

Mr. Budd had spent the rest of the morning fuming and mumbling to Dubber. "The idea" he muttered. "To catch my rabbit and my mockingbird. Can you imagine? The nerve of that brat—!"

"Woof!" said Dubber indignantly. In dog talk, in this case, "woof" meant "outrageous!" Sometimes it meant "terrific!" or "Gee, I'm sorry!" or just "I'm bored," depending on how Dubber woofed. The dog usually knew what his Mr. Budd needed to hear and provided the most appropriate "woof."

The Old Meadow

Toward noon, however, Mr. Budd's knees began to ache. All the exercise that morning, spanking Alvin and dashing around his vegetable garden, trying not to hurt a one, brought on a bad attack of arthritis. "Lumbago," Mr. Budd called it in his old-fashioned way, but it was up-to-date arthritis—and in the joints especially bad. He sunned his knees in his yard, sitting on his stool with his trousers pulled up, and that helped some —but not enough. Perhaps his noon nap would bring relief, he hoped, as he hobbled inside. It was very hard to fall asleep. But at last he did, helped by Ashley Mockingbird, who sang about a sleepy bear who hibernated too early and woke up on New Year's Eve. He couldn't understand the rumpus the winter animals made all around.

But being asleep, Mr. Budd missed the sight, when it appeared.

Ashley flew down from the weather vane and alighted beside Dubber Dog. He'd been exercising his wing since Mr. Budd went inside. "I never seen nothin' like it."

"Me neither." Dubber shook his head. "You better fly down and get Chester and Simon. They wouldn't want to miss this. Oh!—and get Walt, too! This fits right in with his view of humanity. And also"—he lifted his ears quizzically, and then scratched the left one, although it didn't itch—"my flea tells me this is just the beginning."

Ashley took off—sailed, for only a moment—and

Fights!

came down fast, on Chester's log, like an airplane making a very short run.

"Y'all better come upstream," he said. "There's weird things happenin'."

Simon Turtle had been basking—when wasn't he? this time of day—and Chester had been watching a leaf that the brook kept pushing back, although it seemed to be desperate to leave the pool and join the stream. Walt was down below, but he saw the flicker of wings, a flashing that reached down into the depths and made him want to rise.

"What's happening?" the cricket asked.

"Y'all better see for yourselves."

A short while later the friends were hidden inside the shade cast by Mr. Budd's privet hedge.

"You're right," pronounced Simon. "I never did see anything like that." Even Simon had hurried.

"What *do* you think they're doing?" Chester Cricket wondered aloud.

Across the brook were three Irvins on the march, or rather, on the prowl—the same three people that Chester and Ashley had seen just after the Great Debate. Young Alvin, who had recovered remarkably well from his single, mild whop, had gone home and told his father, Allen, and his uncle, Edward, about the ferocious beating that he had just endured. They listened with interest. And so did Alvin's grandma, Malvina.

The Irvins were a picturesque family. Some folk

97

said eccentric. And some field folk said that, after Donald Dragonfly, the Irvins were about as tetched as anyone in the town of Hedley. Malvina ruled the family, both her sons and their wives and her grand-son too, with a rod-of-iron authority. Since reading had always been Malvina's favorite activity—next to ruling —she insisted that her whole family read. Like a lamp in a living room, a passion for reading lit up Malvina Irvin's house.

The passion burnt so bright in her sons that when it came time for them to grow up, instead of becoming insurance salesmen or doctors or lawyers—all honor-able professions—they opened a rare-book shop. Which failed. The Irvin brothers were unsuccessful business-men, although very successful readers. The trouble was, they liked rare books so much that whenever a new shipment came in they could hardly bear to part with a book before they both had pored over it. Many and many a customer had come into the store and asked to buy a particular volume, but either Allen or Edward would shout, "No! no! I haven't finished with that one yet!" In fact, half their stock—they loved the old rare books so much, with their leather bindings that smelled like gravy—they refused to sell at all. But they loaned out some to friends.

Like most dreamers, the Irvins had the idea, as their bookstore was going broke, that one great event would save them both and make them rich. So when Alvin,

Fights!

spanked, came tearfully home and told them what had happened, his father and uncle—and his grandmother —all put their heads together. That was a mistake. For when you add one fuzzy head to another—and then a third—you just get triple fuzziness.

This made the whole situation worse, and started the Irvins off into the meadow. A month ago, a rare book about songbirds had been in a parcel that came from New York. It fascinated both of the brothers—so much that they locked the door to the shop and read it all up in one day. The part that interested them most had to do with mockingbirds. The book said that every now and then a mockingbird came along who could not only mimic, he could improvise, and even create a melody. They were very rare, these mockingbirds, and very valuable. That new bird, the Irvins decided, the one who'd been singing for days on that rickety cabin's weather vane, he must be such a bird.

"Go get him!" ordered Malvina. "Little Alvin had a good idea. A lovely pet. Especially singing in the bookstore window. He'll attract a crowd and they'll buy books—if any are for sale. Now catch him! And none of you gets a bite of supper until that bird is in a cage!"

As Chester watched the three Irvins sneaking stealthily on the opposite side of the brook, he couldn't help asking, "But why are the men wearing dirty clothes?"

Behind bulrushes and marshy shrubs, the two grownup Irvins had on dull, faded green khaki pants and

T-shirts Malvina had forgotten to wash with bleach.

"I think it's so they can fade into the scenery," said Simon.

"Tchoor! That's it! Camouflage. What a couple of meatballs!"

"But with those things hanging over their shoulders?" said Chester. "Fade into the scenery? How——?"

Behind the backs of Allen and Edward, dangling almost to the ground, were two huge butterfly nets. They'd been left over, stored in the attic, from a time in the Irvins' childhood when they'd wanted to collect rare insects. All the butterflies who lived in the meadow were greatly relieved when this phase passed, although the boys never caught a one. They did, however, catch several wasps and were stung accordingly.

"They might as well be dressed up for Halloween," said Dubber.

"Shh!" Chester warned. "They're coming over. I want to see just how far this will go."

With all the stealth and delicacy of two mules and one pony, the Irvins sloshed across the brook. Allen was holding a dish of something, which he set down at the edge of Mr. Budd's vegetable patch. "Here, birdy-birdy-birdy!" he chirped.

An amazed silence fell on the four animals. Then Ashley broke it. "Y'all know somethin'?—I think those jokers are after me! Perhaps I ought to let them catch me—they're so miserable pitiful."

Fights!

"Don't you dare!" said Dubber. "Mr. Budd would have a fit!"

"*Here*—birdy-birdy-birdy," crooned Edward. "Where is it, anyway? It used to sit on the weather vane."

"What's that they're tryin' to catch me with?" whispered Ashley. "Looks like a saucer of corn." He flitted up a twig or two through the privet hedge— then dropped down amazed. "Halloween, did someone say? It's corn *candy* left over from last October most likely!"

"Do you like corn candy, Ashley?" asked Walt.

"Don't know. Never had none." The mockingbird purled a chuckle. "One thing I do know, though—we got goofballs back in West Virginia—believe me, we do!—but you sure got your share in Connecticut, too!"

"Shall I bark?"

"Not yet, rub-a-dub-Dubber! Let's have some fun!" The mockingbird flickered up and perched where he was expected to be. He stuck out his tongue and made a sound that wasn't nearly as musical as most of the sounds he made.

"There he is—!"

"I'll climb up—!"

"Help!" Edward fell from his brother's shoulders. "Ooo! Ow!"

"Be quiet!" urged young Alvin.

Too late.

The Old Meadow

Mr. Budd had been drifting up from his nap. The commotion snapped him wide awake. He roared out of his house like a locomotive, wearing only his underwear. The day had grown hot. "Oh, you Irvins!" But he really did like the Irvins. Especially since that summer, years and years ago, when they'd tried to raise pedigreed Siamese, who all got loose and filled the town of Hedley with pedigreed alley cats. "Two times in one day is too much!"

The fight was unfair. Without much effort, one old man who was overweight and had arthritis proceeded to trounce two men half his age. A good thing did come of it, however: Abner Budd discovered that, in his case at least, righteous indignation could cure arthritis.

"You first!"

Abner whipped a butterfly net over Edward's head. It held him pinned down to his knees and made him look like a crazy beehive, while Mr. Budd marched his brother off—then gave him some hang-gliding help that sent him sprawling into the brook.

"Don't want you to feel neglected."

Then Abner did the same for Edward.

Young Alvin hadn't waited. He was on the other side, shouting for help: his dad and his uncle were being killed.

"This isn't the end, old man!" shouted Edward, as he picked ferns out of his shirt.

"Oh, isn't it?"

Even when the brook was rushy and full, as it was

Fights!

just now from a recent rain, Mr. Budd knew where the stepping-stones were. He'd put them there, before the Irvins had lived in Hedley. Still only clad in his underwear, he flew across the water.

And the sight of this man who treated a stream as if it were the solid earth amazed and terrified the Irvins. They fled home. Where, after an hour of lecturing, Malvina relented and gave them dinner. But she never stopped nagging, and after two hours the Irvin brothers decided that they had to act, if only to silence their mother.

"What a day," murmured Ashley Mockingbird. "Well, I'll have tales to tell—if I ever get back to West Virginia. Mmm-*mm!* What a day!"

This day was not yet over. Events went fast. They often do, if they move at all.

Simon, Walter, and Chester had barely gotten home, ambling slowly through the lavender evening, when, with a whir of wings, the mockingbird appeared again.

"Better come back. Quick."

"Not me." Simon heaved out his breath as he clambered into his muddiest, most comfortable spot. "I've had enough excitement today."

"This here is serious."

"How serious?" Chester Cricket was worried, because Ashley's voice was flat: for once, there was no music in it.

"Better see for yourself." Without waiting for an

103

answer, the mockingbird flew back to Mr. Budd's cabin.

The cricket and the snake followed, fast.

Around the cabin a crowd had gathered. There was Mr. Budd, the Irvin brothers, young Alvin, and even Grandma Malvina. The wives of the Irvin boys stayed home. When Malvina was out, they could watch TV instead of read. There were also three policemen, and that had been Malvina's doing. When her sons and her grandson had gotten home soaked, she decided the family had been humiliated. And the more she lectured her sons, the more insulted the family became. Edward dialed the police station, but insisted that Allen speak and summon the cops.

Malvina hadn't yet decided whether the Irvins should sue Mr. Budd for all his money—not a promising prospect—or just demand an apology. Of one thing she was certain, though: the world must learn that no one could kick her two sons in a brook and get away with it. Someone else's sons, yes, but not hers! She was the only one who could treat them that way.

It was difficult for the officers. As little boys they'd all played in the meadow—they'd all known Mr. Budd —and now they'd been summoned to, maybe, arrest him.

"Mike Gallagher, you should be ashamed!" Mr. Budd poked the chest of the tallest cop. "Coming over here to hassle me—when these goons tried to steal my bird!"

Fights!

"Gee, Mr. Budd—" Mike Gallagher began.

"Don't tell him 'gee'!" Malvina rasped. She had a voice like a draft in a chimney from smoking cigarettes. "Put the handcuffs on him!"

"Mr. Budd," said Mike, and looked off toward the west, toward Avon Mountain, where the lingering rosy light could hide his blush, "you maybe should come downtown with us." He didn't actually take off his handcuffs, which were dangling from his belt, but he touched them.

"Attack, you mutt!" shouted Mr. Budd to Dubber. "Don't you care if these ungrateful bums arrest me? I took burrs out of little Mike Gallagher's hair! If I'm in jail—who'll tend my mockingbird?"

"Oh, we will!" offered Malvina sweetly.

Mr. Budd aimed a kick at Dubber, but missed. Lumbago, or else he changed his mind. "You lazy good-for-nothing you! You hear that? They want to kidnap my bird! Where *were* you the first time these imbecile Irvins came round? Just cowering underneath my hedge! And that darn jay! Because even if you—you dumb dog!—couldn't warn me, at least that blue jay usually shrieks."

That was too much for Dubber: to be told that he'd failed—and like J.J.! When the officers and the Irvins appeared, he'd been munching on a cauliflower. There still were shreds of the white vegetable, spit too, clinging to his lips. In all the excitement and fright— Dubber didn't like either Irvins or cops—he'd

105

forgotten to lick his chops. And the sight of a blue-uniformed human being who might be about to arrest his master made Dubber lose his head. For the first time in years he growled very seriously, and tried to nip Mike Gallagher. But, being Dubber, he missed, of course—just like Mr. Budd—and bit the crease in the officer's pants.

"And look at that!" Malvina wheezed.

"She sounds worse than Simon," whispered Chester.

"A mad dog!" coughed Malvina. "And foam all over his mouth! Call the pound!"

"Can things get any worse?" Walt wondered.

"Yes, they *can!*" said Chester. "And with these human beings—they probably will."

Things did get worse. The officers called the dog pound from a neat little phone that they had in their car. And in fifteen minutes a nice white truck from the pound arrived. It looked like a shrunken ambulance. Two men in clean white suits stepped out, said "Hi," and led Dubber away.

Two men in blue uniforms led Abner Budd to the cop car. He turned, and as Dubber was plodding into his prison on wheels, he tried to shout a few words to his dog. They got trapped in his throat.

SEVEN

Jailbreak—Number One

"We've got to get them out," said Ashley.

John Robin had returned, and all he said was, "They're still in jail. Both of them. A human jail and a dog jail—the pound."

Since he had wings, John Robin had been sent off to spy. Chester Cricket didn't like to use a friend as a spy, but Mr. Budd was gone—Dubber Dog was gone— it had been two days, and those who lived around and under Simon's Pool had to *know!* They were frantic. John Robin, who was familiar with all the byways of the town—he wormed everywhere—seemed to be the answer.

"We do have to get them *out!*" said Walt.

"They'd just put them both back in again," sighed Simon Turtle, with age's weary experience.

There was a round wind blowing, under clouds that were hurrying somewhere. "Round wind" was one of the turtle's favorite expressions. He had used it for years and years. It described a wind—a breeze or a gust, ordinarily, sometimes a steady breath of air—that came from nowhere and everywhere. It blew off the petals of purple irises, shook green reeds, and ruffled the pink of rugosa roses. But everybody, animal and human too, liked the young round wind that circled about them playfully.

John fluffed his feathers. In a round wind, flying was difficult, but he enjoyed being surprised by it. "Simon's right. Those men in uniforms will just come hunting—"

"Tchoor! Of course they'll come hunting, but we can hide them! We've got to get them *out!*" The water got a solid *whop!* It hurt Walter's tail, and the water wasn't changed at all.

"Chester—" began Ashley.

"All right, all right," Chester Cricket agreed. "If they stay in jail too long, they'll turn into half of themselves. Mr. Budd'll be put in an old folks' home—and Dubber—" The cricket refused to think about that. "But how—*how* do we get them out?"

The wind coaxed thoughts on shells, scales, feathers —a cricket's wing—but it whispered no answers.

"Tchoor!" Walter Water Snake suddenly had an idea. "I'll get them out. The thing I've hated all my life is how much the human beings hated *me!* And all us snakes. But now it pays off!" Walt raised up and glowered down onto his friends. "You're lookin' at a deadly serpent! Har! har! I'll scare the guards, and Dubber and Mr. Budd will go free. Simple—?"

Jailbreak—Number One

"Oh, simple!" said Chester. "But how are you going to get to those jails?"

"I'll creep, I'll crawl, I'll slither—if necessary, I'll even writhe! But I hate that word. And I'll get directions first. John Robin—where *is* the pound? I'll rescue Dubber before Mr. Budd. They take less time to dispose of dogs than men. John—where?"

"No problem," said John. "You go six blocks on Mountain Road, take a left at Fisk, and then two blocks, hook a right at Hedley Avenue, but only one block, left at Santell, three blocks, then half a block on Salter Street—and there you are!"

"You see?" Walter splashed some water at Chester. "Not a thing in the world could be more simple!"

"Oh, nothing," the cricket agreed heartily. "But Walt—let me ask you this—have you ever been out of this meadow before?"

"I crossed Mountain Road once. The grass in front of the Andersons' house looked so nice for basking."

"Oh, that's a real long journey, all right!"

"And I'm good at north and south—stuff like that," Walter Water Snake insisted. "I've made up my mind! Here I go—"

A silence held everyone still. It was full of both wonder and fear: Walter Water Snake was venturing out—way outside the meadow. The round wind had spun itself out into nothing by now. All the animals watched as Walt flicked his tail to wave goodbye—not a care in the world—and slithered off.

"That's the wrong way, Walt!" John Robin chirped. "Mountain Road is over there."

"Oh." Walter lifted his head and swung it around like a broken compass. "Don't worry, you guys—I have an infallible sense of direction."

"Tchoor—we all can see," muttered Chester despondently, as Walter began once more the most important writhe of his life. "John—follow him! And fly above him. Try to chirp him the right way."

"Okay."

The afternoon wore on. Then twilight wore on. Then evening wore on. And everyone tried not to show by a word or a cough or a quick look off toward Mountain Road that this day was becoming difficult. But when dark night took hold of the world, everybody gave up pretending and settled down to be downright scared—and in public at that. The night was very cloudy too, and the moon, almost full, was just a pale eye in the sky.

"Where *are* they?" The cricket, at last, couldn't stand it. "It's been hours and hours!"

"The pound is a long way off," Simon Turtle tried to remind him.

"I've done my darndest! I've done my best!" Without anyone noticing him—a robin can be so subtle, and especially in the dark—John had settled on Chester's log. "And I lost him."

"John—"

Jailbreak—Number One

"I got him to Fisk—but then it got dark—and Walter blends in with the dark—and also, the humans were going home—horns honking—the horrible sounds humans make when day's over—their radios blaring! He couldn't hear my chirp any more!"

"John—stop now," said Chester. "Nobody blames you."

"I do," said John Robin, and choked. "I've been looking and looking—under every streetlight—and chirping till my throat is sore! The wings, too. I'll barely make it back to my nest. And what Dorothy will say—me coming back at this hour—I can't even imagine." Poor John was winded. His wing muscles ached, those miracle things that let him fly. And he felt guilty too, for having lost Walter. "I'm sorry," his voice drooped sadly down. "I tried, but—"

"Shh! Hush!" Simon interrupted. "I hear panting."

"Huh-huh—!"

"There it is again!"

"I don't hear anything," said John, but one note in his voice was hope.

"Hush again! Someone's blundering through those bulrushes—?

"If it's blundering," said John Robin, "it's got to be—"

"*Dubber!*" Chester shouted—squeaked, shrieked. He made the loudest sound ever heard from one lone Connecticut cricket. "You're back!"

"Let me get to the pool! Let me get to the pool—"

"Come on, houn' dog," Ashley Mockingbird encouraged him. "It's right here—"

"Not for me—"

Around Dubber's neck, the animals saw, was what looked like a ruined shoelace. "Oooo-*ssss!*" it hissed pathetically.

"That's him!" said John Robin. "My found-again friend!"

"Let go, Walt," Dubber encouraged. "We're home."

With the weakest of "plops" the water snake dropped head first in the pool.

"He's awfully dry!" Dubber counseled the others. "You've got to be patient."

"What *happened?*" asked Chester.

"Yes—after I lost him—what—?"

"Wait. Just wait now. I want Walt to tell it."

The water snake stayed below for a worrying long time. No bubbles came up, no ripples to show that anyone was alive down there—just the pale echo of a moon smudge on the surface.

"You better go get him, Simon," said Chester.

"No need," said Simon.

A head emerged from the depths. Then from that black head there emerged a long and luxurious sigh: "Oh, water—"

"Welcome back," said Chester. "I take it that city life didn't agree—"

"Oh, water!" crooned Walter Water Snake. He

addressed all his friends, sounding very much like his old self. "Have any of you sweet field folk here ever thought of the beauty of water?"

"Where *were* you?" asked John, who wanted not to feel so guilty.

"Wet brook of my heart! I will never leave you again!"

"Walt—"

"Yes, water is my true home! It's all around—it's up and down—it's here and there—when you're in it, water is everywhere!" In a fit of relief, Walter kissed the surface of Simon's Pool. Walter's Pool now, too. "I love you, water." He slurped up some. "It tastes good, too! Oh, water—!"

"What happened?" hollered Chester.

"The cool comfort of water bathes every scale. If you're lucky enough to have scales," said Walt.

"I really am going to get mad," Chester Cricket decided.

"Anyway," said Walt, and his zig-zags in the pool suggested a story with lots of twists and turns, "fearlessly I went out into a world of concrete, bricks and cement, guided only by a robin—who soon took off through fear of the dark."

"I did not!"

"Who soon got lost, through no fault of his own, in the gloaming."

"That's better."

The Old Meadow

"It's a horrible world of sidewalks, curbstones, and gutters. But one thing it taught me: *I was not made for hard surfaces!*"

"That's big-eared news," said Robert Rabbit, who'd added himself to the group without anybody noticing.

"Despite John Robin's excellent directions—but you've got to admit, birds have it easy—I found myself lost."

"It's a wonder you found yourself in Connecticut at all!" said John.

"I almost wasn't," said Walt. "I got to a part of town where there were no houses. So, logically, I decided that I'd taken a wrong road somewhere. I turned right around—my stomach scales were pretty sore by now—and inched my way back toward the lights of Hedley. And here I'll omit certain incidents. Like the driver of that big Mack truck who tried to run over me three times. And the old lady tending her garden at twilight. How nice, I thought. But she caught a glimpse of me—that lady has *problems!*—and started screaming, 'Snake! Snake! Snake!'—and went after me with a shovel, as if her last dahlia depended on it. You'd have thought I was King Cobra. Why *do* the humans hate us so much. Oh, well—"

Walt took another deep dip. "I will not go into all those ordeals, because when I was about to give up and try to become a garter snake—in *somebody's* garden! since I thought I'd never get home again—I heard a sound that lifted my heart."

Jailbreak—Number One

"Music?" asked Chester.

"No. Yowling dogs. I knew I must be near the pound. And I even thought I could pick out the pot-bellied bellowing of our dearest Dubber Dog. My buddy!"

"But it wasn't me," Dubber explained. "I'd fallen asleep from hopelessness. It was a Saint Bernard named Siegfried."

"But it was *dogs!*" Walter declared. "And lots of 'em—all cooped up. It had to be the pound. I made for the noise—" Walt flashed under water, flashed up in the air, and flashed all over the calm pool's surface.

Drops of silver, which the moon reached to touch, fell on top of everyone. No one cared. Not even dry Donald Dragonfly, who'd added himself to the gathering, too. "It's different," he murmured to himself, as he shook his wings. "It's annoying—but it may be a blessing, too. I like drops of water."

Walter's head puzzled this way and that. "But this is what's weird. They could have been expecting me, the dogcatchers. There could have been a sign outside saying, *Welcome Walter Water Snake!* The door was wide open!"

"Of course it was," said Chester. "It's a summer night—they left the door open to get some air."

"Oh. Yes. Well—that fits. You're logical, Chester C. Anyway, without the use of fangs as yet, I slipperyed right in—and what did I see?"

"I know." Robert Rabbit's sympathizing voice sank low.

So did Donald's soft buzz. "Rows and rows of puppies in cages!"

"Not exactly," said Walt. "The dogcatchers were watching television! I slipped silently past them—three of them—and they were all so fascinated by who killed whom, and with what, that not a one of them saw a scale."

"But *I* did, Walt!" Dubber Dog's pride bubbled in his voice. "I saw you right away."

"Sure you did!" said Walt. "The gunshots on the TV woke you up."

"I would've woken up anyhow."

"I saw the cages—D.D. was on the lowest shelf—and I saw him! I saw the bolt, and I knew that I could nose it out, ease it out, if only I could get the chance. But then I also saw, to my sorrow, that the barking of those mutts—"

"I don't much like that word," rumbled Dubber.

"I also saw that my snake's presence in the pound had caused those lovable canine creatures to howl even louder—and the three dogcatchers, distracted from *Murder in Manhattan*, had begun to wonder what was up. I knew this moment was do or dry up. I coiled myself—and I don't like to coil—and gave a loud gargle. But I was so dry, just breathing would do. And I shook my tail. Get it—?" Walter beamed on his friends. "Instant rattlesnake! You just add water—or rather, you take it away—and you've got a venomous serpent: *me!*" Walt sighed. "It's so sad. Nobody trusts anyone. But it worked. The three TV freaks took off like rockets, and I very much doubt if they've landed yet. I shinnied up to the bolt on Dubber's cage, gave it a push—one free mutt. Beg pardon, Dubber: one free canine."

"But that isn't all he did!" interrupted Dubber. "Tell the rest, Walt—tell!"

Walt hung his head, in becoming modesty. "My kindness overcame me. I freed *all* the dogs! And such a joyous yowling and howling was never heard before."

"But now I come in!" gurgled Dubber again. " 'Cause the ruckus of us animals, pouring out in the street, was like something never heard before, I said, 'Let's go, Walt! While we can.' Walt said, 'I can't. My tummy scales—! Goodbye, old friend. This is farewell.' "

"Walt said *that*—?"

"Yes, he did!" said Dubber. "Then *I* had my idea! I don't have too many—but some of the ones I have are darn good. I said—why didn't he wrap himself around me like a collar—and I'd run him home lickety-split!"

"Which he did! The darling dog—!" Walt leaned over and gave Dubber Dog a kiss on his buttony nose. Then he butted the buttony nose with his head, so as

117

not to seem too sentimental. "And I'm here to tell all you field folk—I will never bite this dog again! He's a hero—as my tummy scales can testify!"

"But, Walt," Dubber chuckled, "you never did bite me."

"Well, then—I'll never even threaten," said Walt.

A good feeling of fellowship went round and round the pool. The moon had cleared, too.

"So we've got one back," said Simon Turtle. He liked the friendship—the moonlight, as well—but he lived among real things. Mud. Irises. Thunderstorms. Ragusa roses. And the fact of jail. "How about Mr. Budd?"

"The team of Dubber and Walt will rescue him, too!"

"It won't be so easy," Chester was thinking. "A dog—a wanted dog, at that—even without a snake collar—is still a dog. But a man?"

"I'll go alone!"

"With that tender tummy?" asked Chester.

"How long are y'all, Walt?"

"Besides—you'd get lost. The human pound is much farther into the center of Hedley than the dog jail is."

"How much do—I mean, you're in great shape!— but—how much do you weigh?"

The good partnership of happiness that the animals shared began to loosen.

"Please excuse these personal questions, but—"

"I have got to get to that jail!" said Walter. "Maybe tummy scales can be replaced."

"Tchoor!" said Chester. "And so can my wings and antennae!"

"How *heavy* are you, Walter?" the mockingbird demanded to know.

Snake looked at bird. Without the Truce, it would have been murder. But now, like a spark or a star, a flicker of hope was kindled.

"You have an idea?" Walter Water Snake asked, but skeptically.

Ashley sang one of his most private tunes. "I do." Then he added several flourishes to it. "It just might work, too—the Good Lord willin' an' the creek don't rise."

EIGHT

A Singing Lesson

"No use," panted Ashley. "You're just too fat. And long."

"I'm trying, *hard,* to be thin!" said Walter. "And short!"

"We're all doing the best we can." John Robin had collapsed halfway down Chester's log. This strange experiment was taking place on—and was also supposed to take off from—the log. "Two birds just aren't enough."

"Trouble is—we're not big and strong," said Ashley. "Let's try 'er one more time. Was I grabbin' too tight with my claws?"

"No, no," said Walter, who was stretched straight along the log, in the easiest position for a robin and a mockingbird to grasp him and grapple him into the air. "What is pain, when I'm making history? The first water snake to fly! And also the last, I suspect."

For that was the idea: John Robin and Ashley Mockingbird would fly Walt Snake to the human jail. The trouble was—they weren't husky enough, despite the fact that Walter had tried to lose weight overnight.

"Here we go!" cheered Ashley.

And there they went—for three feet. Then the two birds had to let go their grasp. The whole weird cluster of birds and snake was plunging toward Simon's Pool. Claws opened—snake fell.

Walter came up with no complaint at all. "That's the nice thing about all this history-making." He smiled happily, and lounged on his back around the pool. "When the victim gets dropped, he falls right were he lives—into comfortable water."

"I've got to talk to him." Ashley settled next to the opening to Chester's home.

"But he hates you," said the cricket. "He's jealous. And he doesn't like Mr. Budd—"

"I've got to talk to him."

"—and you might have another fight. He *is* strong, too—from beating up all the little birds."

"That's why I've got to talk to him. Where's he likely to be?"

"In his beech tree," said Chester. "When J.J.'s mad, or when he sulks, he has to be in that beech tree alone. He chases everyone—even those dim-witted sparrows —and they *like* him! And there he sits, like an angry king who was just forced to quit."

"Where's the beech tree, Chester?"

"If you make for the northwest corner of the

meadow, you can't help but see it. It's the brightest, most beautiful tree in that part. Except when J.J.'s sulking there."

"I'll see y'all, then," said the mockingbird. And most birds would have just chirped "bye"—but Ashley favored his friends with a song that lasted almost half a minute. They never forgot it.

There was no mistaking the bright beech tree. It rose up in the splendid noon like a castle of wood—a castle that had a few battlements falling. But even the dead branches, hanging down, seemed beautiful in their decay. In the center of it, where the trunk forked apart, sat J. J. Bluejay, all alone. And he seemed, as Chester had said, like a sad deserted king on his throne.

"Ha, J.J.!" said Ashley, as he alighted. "Will I get busted up if I sit here a spell?"

"Oh—I guess not." J.J. made a big show of moving over. "And why do you say that? 'Ha?'—like that. It's 'hi!' "

"The way I talk, J.J. In the South—"

"Well, you're *not* in the South!" J.J. begrudged the inches he'd moved and crowded Ashley against the trunk. "And we say 'you'—'*you!*'—not 'yuh.' "

"I sometimes even say—'y'all!' "

In the mockingbird's unblinking black eyes there was something that could have been laughter, or teasing, or just simply news about how a mockingbird talks.

J.J. glanced at him and lifted a wing. But the light coming down, filtered green through the leaves, made him feel uncertain—was he being ridiculed again? Or not? And he folded his wing back into position.

"Tell y'all what," said Ashley. "How about if *you* teach me how to talk—an' I'll teach *you* how to sing?"

J.J. jerked his head toward Ashley in startled disbelief. Then he squawked cynically. *"Aw, haw!* With this voice? I've been told—by some of my best friends, too—that I sound like a dead branch falling off."

"Not so!" said Ashley. "You've got one nice song— 'Doodly-do' when you bob your head."

"Oh, that!" scoffed J.J. "All blue jays can do that! And I don't do it very well."

"I don't think y'all do it enough. Beg pardon—you just 'awk' and 'erk' too much. Can I tell you a story?"

"Oh—I guess so." J.J. cleaned his right wing with his beak, as if he had much more important things to do than listen to stories.

"This tale could be called," Ashley Mockingbird started, *"The Peeper Who Couldn't Peep."* An' it happened to me. 'Bout a year ago, last spring, I was up much later than usual. The full moon just made me happy, an' I had to stay awake an' sing. Well, in between songs I heard this pitiful little *'eep!'* I flew toward it, an' there, in a marsh, I found this peeper. Y'all have peepers here, J.J.?"

"Sure we do!" said the blue jay, who was very interested in the story by now. "Those tiny frogs—they're the only sign of spring I trust."

"Me, too! Well, there the pitiful critter was, clingin' onto a bulrush—an' he didn't know how to peep! 'Course, when he first saw me, he got all riled up, me bein' a bird, 'cause he thought I was goin' to gobble him down. But though there's no Truce in West Virginia, I never would have done it. Poor Joey was just so miserable and little! That's what his name was—Joey Peeper." Ashley took a glance at J.J. "I squawked at him not to be scared—"

"You squawked—" J.J. disbelieved.

"Sure I squawked! I always squawk, when the feathers are ruffled the wrong way. Or when somebody thinks I'm goin' to eat him. Anyways, after many attempts—durin' some of which I tried to show off—I taught that peeper how to peep!"

"Really?"

"Just one chirp—like Chester's—was all I had to imitate. Then little Joey did it so well that all the other peepers stopped peepin' an' listened."

"How wonderful!"

"Him an' me peeped together all night long. 'Till that fuzzy blue came over the ridges of the mountains where our people live."

This little story—for a reason J. J. Bluejay didn't quite understand—just broke his heart. And then mended it again. "Little Joey." J.J. lived through the tale again. "I wouldn't have eaten him either."

"An' I'm here to tell you"—Ashley made his voice stern—"I'm not flyin' off this branch till I've taught you, J. J. Bluejay, to sing! If Joey can learn, so can you!"

"Do you think so?" Like the golden-green light that fell on his feathers, hope bathed the blue jay. "Me—?"

"You! An' we'll start with the hardest thing: a trill. Now listen—" And Ashley trilled. It was as if two wings were sound, and one beat like a flicker of gold— then the other beat, just a little bit different, but also gold. Yet silver, too. It was as if—they were both so quick and so close together—it was almost as if they both were one. "It's like—"

J.J. interrupted. He lifted his wing, but timidly now, and rested it on the the mockingbird. "Stop."

"What—?"

"I want to apologize. I hit you—"

"J.J.—I had it due. A show-offy thing like me—" The mockingbird took one quick look, then yanked his eye from the blue jay's eyes. "If somebody has a gift —I'm not sayin' I do—but he shouldn't ever use it to make someone else feel small. Now—about the trill—"

Ashley cleared his throat and trilled again. The blue jay's wing on his own wing felt good. It even entered into the trill. "Two notes—see? But even *your* throat don't know which is which."

J.J.'s first attempt at a trill—but of course he was

very nervous, and went too slow, and lost his breath—
his first try sounded like a sick sparrow.

"Mhmm," said Ashley, who had perfect pitch. To
hear something like that made his head and heart ache.
"I think if you had some spit in your throat—spit's very
important—"

J.J. tried again, with good spit in his throat. And
then something did sound. It wasn't a trill, but it
wasn't a dead branch falling off.

"It won't work," J.J. laughed. "And, Ashley—I don't
care!"

"But I do!" exclaimed Ashley, amazed. Only laughter could bring out J.J.'s trill. And there was a real
trill in the blue jay's unguarded happiness. "Y'all do it
again! I'll die on this branch unless I hear you trill
again!"

J.J. trilled. "Okay? Or would you rather have
'awk' 'squawk'?"

"J.J., I do believe you're developin' a sense of
humor! And remember—good laughter's the happiest
sound there is."

"You're being so nice," said the jay, "I wish there
was something that I—"

"We'll go into that later. Let's try some scales!"

A scale is a little run of notes that go up or down,
depending on which way you're headed. J.J.'s voice
tried to head down first, and even Ashley, polite as he
was, couldn't hide a wince. For J.J.'s descending scale

127

sounded as if a terrified child had fallen downstairs and screamed as he hit every step.

"Pretty bad, huh, Ashley?"

"Oh, it has promise!" But the only promise that *that* scale had was—the child just might live, with luck. "Let's try 'er goin' up."

By some dreadful miracle, it now sounded as if that unfortunate child had managed to fall upstairs.

"Let's quit! I'm hopeless!"

"J.J.—we are *not* gonna quit! It may frazzle every leaf on this tree, but you will sing a scale!"

Although they all shuddered a bit, not one leaf fell from the great beech before J.J. got his scales, both the up one and the down. That speaks a great deal about the strength of beeches. By working his "Doodly-oo" sound in, the bluejay softened his grating 'awk-awk' —and Ashley was satisfied at last.

"Creek didn't rise, either," murmured Ashley, who was happy and dazed at the wonder of what was possible.

"All right now, mockingbird—let's have it!" The sparkle was in the blue jay's eye now.

"Have what?" asked Ashley innocently. But inside his chest his small, hardy, reliable heart was beating with pride—not at J.J.'s scales, but at the thought that the blue jay could now make fun of someone without wanting to hurt. "Y'all think *I* have ulterior motives in teachin' a fellow bird to sing?"

A Singing Lesson

"I *do* think that—yes!" said J.J. A squawk of the blue jay's new laughter came out. "So let's have it!"

"Well—" And Ashley began to explain.

A few minutes later, two eager friendly birds had settled on Chester's log.

"Here's the fourth member of the plot!" Ashley Mockingbird was in the midst of a big adventure. He knew it, too. And anyone could see, from the shuddering in his wings, he wanted to share it with everyone.

Walt reared up and stared at J.J. "Will you behave?"

"Ah'm a new bird!"

"What? 'Ah'm'? This blue jay's gone crazy—!"

"Let's don't waste time, Walt." The mockingbird had taken over. "We ought to practice. John's got to take your head—since he knows the crisscrossy streets of this town. J.J. gets your middle—you're heaviest there—"

"Thanks a lot!"

"—an' I get your tail. I'll just follow along, with as much of you as I can."

Walt poked his face at the mockingbird now. "All of me, I hope!"

Ashley burbled a laugh. "All or nothin'!"

"Oh, gosh!" said Dubber Dog, who'd been sitting on the bank. "I wish I could help! Can't I go, too?"

"Tchoor!" said Walt. "We'll get thirty-five eagles, who aren't afraid of fleas—maybe they can get you off

129

the ground. I don't mean it, Dubber, ol' pal." He darted up and made himself into a snakeskin dog collar, around Dubber's neck. Very dashing, he looked. "Your fleas are my fleas—and partner, I am proud to have them! But the thing is, to get Mr. Budd out now. You're a fugitive yourself, remember."

"Oh, I know," Dubber gloomed, and gathered his haunches under him. "But I worry and worry."

"Of course," said Walt. "With a wrinkly, furry brow like yours, what else could you do?"

Walt dropped off of Dubber's neck, stretched himself on the grass of the bank, and shouted, "Okay, guys —time! Let's try it up here, since there's three of you. Makes a better runway."

The three birds flew up into position: head, middle, and tail. They all felt a little strange. Without saying so out loud, each one wondered if any three birds—any birds at all—had tried to fly a snake before. In friendship that is. Walt took a last look at Simon's Pool. Beneath and around its flickering blue-green surface he'd had his home for so long. "Mr. Budd has his cabin, and Chester his log, but I have you, pool," Walter Water Snake murmured.

"Come on, birds!" he shouted. "Let's up and at 'em!"

"But anyway"—a thought had just plodded through Dubber Dog's mind—"if you do get him out, well, what'll we do then? With Mr. Budd? And me, too! We'll just be escaped criminals."

A Singing Lesson

"Will you shut up, you mutt?" hissed Walt.

"We'll worry about that later," said John.

"Go tidy up the cabin—you fur-lined idiot!" said J.J.

"Leave bad enough alone," advised Ashley. "We're off!"

With a flurry of wingbeats that flattened grass, raised dust, made Chester's and Simon's eyes blink, the strange contraption left the ground. But the first trial of this airborne invention, made up of three birds and one water snake, was not too successful. The birds were out of flap: their wings didn't beat together. Walter felt a jiggling, then wobbling—a lurching—he swayed from side to side—and then, without saying goodbye, the birds loosened their claws. Birds are terrified of crashing, and at the last moment they had to fly free, alone, and save themselves.

Walter fell in a fern bed beside the brook. He hurt, in the lower part of his back, but he made up his mind, right there in the ferns, that this was a day for heroism. "It's all right, you guys!" he called up. Just twenty-five broken bones, he wondered—but only to himself.

The three birds flew round and round, apologizing in the air. They all felt guilty, swooping down and soaring up, as they tried to get back their composure. A bird doesn't like to fail—even when he's trying to fly a snake. They settled beside Walt, who was soothing himself in the ferns.

"Just, next time," said Walt, "water would be best.

Next mud, heaps of grass—but for a snake's sake, don't drop me on Mountain Road. It's hard! Off we go again! And by the way, let me count, like they do in a rowboat, so you'll all beat your wings in sync."

The flying machine assembled itself once again. Walt said, "Okay! I'm thinking airy thoughts now— I'm light!—I'm a feather! *Flap* two three—and *flap* two three—"

He happened to glance down, and his breath stopped in his throat. The birds, however, who were used to this view, had gotten the beat and went on flapping rhythmically.

"Oh, look!" Walt exclaimed. "We're flying."

Below him, Pasture Land, Tuffet Country, the course of the brook as it flowed past Chester's ruined old home, the battered old stump, in the north J.J.'s beech and a growth of untended trees, in the south the paths the Town Council had planned, and even—when Walter looked under and behind—the shimmer of Simon's Pool: Walt's whole world was below. And every single part, like a piece in a jigsaw puzzle, fitted into every other part. And Mr. Budd's cabin. It, too, appeared to Walter's eyes and seemed to fit in, and make the whole meadow complete.

"Once more!" Walter shouted. "But lower and slower."

His wings obeyed, and below him his world spun under again. "Oh-ah—" For the first time in his life, Walter Water Snake was speechless.

The Old Meadow

On the ground, a few field folk saw him. Not many. Few animals expected a snake to appear in the sky.

"That's Walter!" said Emily Chipmunk.

"And flying!" said her brother, Henry.

The fussy chipmunks were cleaning their front yard, as usual.

"He shouldn't be up there."

"No," Henry said, sighing. He was sick of cleaning. "But sometimes I wish that I was."

Ms. Beatrice Pheasant also saw the flight. She only gave it a glance. *"Hmm!"* she sniffed, as the water snake soared through the heavens above her. "Some people just never know their place!"

Donald Dragonfly lay on his twig. The brook hurried beneath him. He was just about to take a nap, when something happened in the sky.

"Hi, Don! Hi, Don!"

Donald sleepily looked up.

"Come on up and join me!"

"I flew this morning, Walter," said Don. But something bothered the dragonfly. He cradled his head on his twig again. Walter Water Snake was up in the sky. It did seem strange. But not so strange that it kept him awake.

"I'm flying!" hollered Walter Water Snake down.

"Well, that's nice," mumbled Donald. He dreamed about wings—not his own—that day.

"Oh, flying!" Walter said to his wings. "We all belong up here!"

A Singing Lesson

"*We* do!" said John Robin. "We're birds! We do this all the time."

Crestfallen in heaven, Walter said, "All right. Let's —oh, wait! Once over there—"

There was a single human being who saw this rickety miracle. Young Alvin Irvin had been wandering, alone, near Mr. Budd's cabin. He was wondering if he'd done the right thing—that is, getting his father and uncle involved—and he also felt dismal. As if the world was a boring and disappointing place—full of grandmothers. Then above him he saw—

"Hooray for snakes!"

"Do you hear that?" Walt said to his wings. "For two years that kid has been trying to bean me with rocks. And now he's shouting 'Hooray for snakes!' Fly over him—*near!* I want him to know that I like him. Despite the rocks."

Wings did as they were told.

"I'm awfully tired already," puffed John.

"All right, my fellows," said Walter Water Snake, "I've seen my home as it ought to be. From above. Now let's go to jail."

NINE

Jailbreak—Number Two

Chester Cricket decided that waiting was the worst torment of all. It was worse than a flood in the brook. It was even worse than one of the sudden meadow fires that swept through Pasture Land, after days and days without rain. The human beings caused most of them, but sometimes lightning did, too. But waiting, not knowing, the fearful endless wondering—that had to be the worst. Yesterday the cricket had waited for Dubber Dog; today for Mr. Budd.

"It's really too much," Chester said to himself, as he fidgeted on top of his log. "I'm only an insect, after all. I ought to be chirping merrily—not a care in the world."

The glowing golden late afternoon didn't help one bit. There had been a brief thunderstorm about half an hour after that marvelous flying machine made of birds and serpent had vanished into the southern sky.

"They could have been struck by lightning!" said Chester. "Blasted all to smithereens!—the four of them."

Jailbreak—Number Two

"What?" mumbled Dubber. He'd fallen into a nervous doze.

"I was talking to myself."

"Then why talk so loud? Can't you hear yourself?"

"Oh, go back to sleep!"

"No, don't!" said Simon. He eased his head out from under his shell just as far as it could go. "Don't sleep!" he rasped, with an urgency unusual for a turtle. "Hide, dog!"

Silently, on the fat pads of his paws, Dubber sneaked down the bank and concealed himself in a clump of reeds.

Two men were approaching on the path that led to the brook. It wound down from the hill where Bill Squirrel lived in his maple tree—his first tree, an elm, had been smitten by blight—past Simon's Pool, then crossed the brook on stepping-stones and went on to Mr. Budd's cabin. The town Councilmen, who'd voted to preserve the Old Meadow, thought stepping-stones were a lovely touch—so natural and quaint. However, these stepping-stones weren't like Mr. Budd's. His were *stones*. These were made of concrete.

"He couldn't be anywhere else," said one man. "They always go home. No place else to go. Especially the dopy, soulful ones, with eyes like that pooch."

"Yeah, but if he isn't there, in that cabin—"

In his hole in the log, with all his small heart, Chester Cricket willed—*Dubber Dog, don't move! Or make a sound!*

137

"Then we'll come back tomorrow. They always go home. He won't have a home to go too much longer. Those old fogies from the Council said a vicious dog and a senile old man are good reasons to pull the hut down. They've been looking for reasons. And now they got them. The pooch has to be lurking somewhere."

"Yeah—and *we've* got to catch him. You know what those guys said: we catch all the dogs that escaped—and we've only got six—or no job!"

"We'll come back tomorrow. He's sure to be here. Where's the old guy, by the way?"

"In jail. They're trying to decide where to send him. There's a lot of old folks' places that won't take him. No money."

The first man—his name was Moe Saffer, and he had one son and two daughters—paused. He looked ahead. Through an opening in the trees he saw the cabin that he was going to have to ransack, for a dog. "You know something, Dennis. I used to play here a lot. 'Course, I was little then."

"Me, too." Moe's partner, Dennis Reynolds chuckled —but somewhat ruefully. "One Halloween, I remember, I came all the way here. And none of the kids would come with me. But Mr. Budd—I think he'd been waiting—he had some candy. He said, 'Well, Dennis Reynolds!—thank goodness you're here, at least. No one else came.' And then he filled up my bag with candy."

Jailbreak—Number Two

"Let's get on with it," said Moe. He shivered. Perhaps there was a chill in the air. "The Old Meadow is full of my childhood. It makes me feel—creepy—"

"Yeah. Me, too," said Dennis.

The two men stepped carefully, but not with pleasure: they had to use those artificial concrete stones. Mr. Budd's hut was this side of the brook.

"You see! You see! They're going to ship him off!"

"Now calm down, Dubber," said Chester. "They were looking for you—"

"But they're talking about Mr. Budd—"

Dubber Dog had lumbered up out of the rushes, and now seemed about to have a fat fit. Red sunset flamed over Avon Mountain, but the brilliant colors on his coat just made him seem more wild—mad!

"They're trying to find a place for him. You know what that means: a place—a 'home'—a little room somewhere."

"Dubber, please calm down—"

"No, I won't calm down! I'll—I'll—I don't know *what* I'll do! But I'll terrorize the world! And I'll shake up the whole Old Meadow! Potbelly or not."

"I'm back."

In the frenzy, jowls shaking and hackles raised, of Dubber's fury, nobody had noticed John Robin alighting without a sound on the log.

"The others will be here later. It's much harder," John Robin explained, with a confidential chirp, "when one of the group is an old man walking. And with a snake in his pocket at that." He warbled a giggle.

"What *happened!*" shouted Chester. It seemed to him that for two whole days that was all he'd been able to say.

"Why don't you just wait." John laughed at his private joke. "You'd never have guessed where Walter is hiding. Nobody would."

"Oh, waiting! Waiting! I'm going crazy! I just wish I had some big fangs, like Walt. I *would* bite somebody!"

For more than an hour, Chester fumed. And fidgeted. And shifted from one set of legs to the other. That was one of the great advantages of being a cricket: when you were so nervous you had to shift legs, you had a lot of legs to shift.

The wait wasn't all that boring, however. A long half hour after John Robin had flitted off to tell his mate, Dorothy, that he was safe, flashlights appeared on the hill above the pool.

"Run, Dubber!" said Chester. "It's the dogcatchers again. Go hide in the woodsy part."

"Let me know if Mr. Budd—"

"Get going!"

Dubber loped off to the northwest corner of the Old Meadow, where nature had been left to itself. J.J.'s beech was there, too. There were no paths where the human beings could stroll—no benches where anyone could sit. It was the part all the animals loved best. And trees, bushes, and brambles made hiding easy—if not comfortable.

But it wasn't the dogcatchers who came down from the hill, the bright rays in their hands darting everywhere. In the thickening darkness Chester hadn't been able to see too well, but as the men tripped and felt their way down, he saw uniforms: the police. The shafts of their flashlights, crisscrossing each other, seemed like baffled eyes that couldn't focus. Their blue uniforms glimmered dark in the night.

"Blue shines on my wings nice, too," murmured Donald Dragonfly, all by himself. He was always creeping up, unobserved. "But I don't want to wear a uniform."

"Hush, Donald," whispered Chester.

"He's gotta go back to that cabin."

They're treating Mr. Budd just like Dubber, thought Chester. A man—a dog. What a town!

"Who says so? After what I've seen today, I don't believe anything!"

"You scared?"

"I'm not scared. Who's scared. But that kind of a snake—in Connecticut! My wife'll have a fit, if I tell her."

"Then don't. The exterminators must have got the snake out by now."

"We'll search the cabin. Then, if he's not there—"

"—we'll go back to the station house. But after we've

called the exterminators, to make sure they were there."

"Right. I just hope he's still wearing my coat. It's gotten sort of chilly." This voice sounded like Mike Gallagher.

"And listen—snakes—all kinds of snakes—are scared of lights, aren't they? Like the light from a flashlight."

"Sure."

"Tchoor!" echoed Chester Cricket, inside his hole. He jumped straight around and hid his head in the pile of grass that he used for a bed. And no policeman heard his laughter, as he wondered about this new kind of snake.

Then there was more waiting. But this time it was sort of exciting. The cops trudged off, toward Mr. Budd's cabin, darting their flashlights left and right on the way, in search of a deadly species of snake that had just been seen in Connecticut. Chester's waiting, although it was still a bit anxious, began to feel like fun. There were more adventures to be told, and retold.

The moon, one day from the full, rose over the world like a silver promise that had to be kept. The hand of a cloud was barely concealing one cheek of it. And Chester Cricket decided that he would stay awake forever before he'd not know what was happening.

"Ha, Chester!" said Ashley Mockingbird.

"Oh! I didn't even hear you. Where's Mr. Budd—Walt—J.J.—?"

Jailbreak—Number Two

"All here. Mr. Budd's on the other side of the brook. He's a wonder! May be old and overweight, but he's got a lot of grace—for a man."

Mr. Budd was sloshing across now. He hated those concrete stepping-stones and refused to use them. Puffing a little, he rested on the bank. Chester stared—and couldn't believe what he saw. Mr. Budd was wearing a deep-blue coat, an officer's coat. It was spick-and-span clean. His pants, too, looked strangely well-pressed.

J. J. Bluejay settled on Mr. Budd's shoulder.

"We're back," sighed Abner.

J.J. tried his trill. There was peace between former enemies.

"Poor Walt, though," Ashley sadly murmured. "He got lost in the rush for freedom." But his mockingbird's sigh was too gloomy to be the truth.

"He did *not!*" said the cricket. "Walter Water Snake, you come out of there!" He'd seen a wiggle inside the blue coat.

A head peeked out of the deep right pocket of Mr. Budd's new officer's coat. "Who told? It must have been John. Robins never know when to shut up!" Walter slithered out all the way and plunged down straight into the pool.

Mr. Budd shouted, "Hey! Wait—snake! I got to thank you!" He looked up at the moon, and then around at the whole Old Meadow, as if seeing things for the first—or last—time.

The Old Meadow

Walter surfaced, silently. He wanted to hear what Mr. Budd said.

But all Abner said was, "I don't care now—and I don't even know what's happened—but this last night I just want to be home."

The police, the dogcatchers—they all had gone. Now its rightful owner went back to his cabin.

"I'd just like to see my dog once more," Mr. Budd plodded off in the night. And he needed no light, although the moon was there. He'd walked that path for fifty-nine years.

"I want to know—" began Chester.

"Me and my six-winged kadoodle," said Walt, "lounged over the town of Hedley, enjoying the many sights below—"

"I'm not going to get angry," Chester Cricket reminded himself. He tried to think of a lullaby. None came to mind. "But if this darned snake—!" His antennae were sticking up like hatpins. *"What happened!"* he squeaked.

"I'm telling you! I enjoyed the many sights below, like streetlights going on, houselights, too. From the sky it all looked like David Spider's web—but made out of lights. And husbands coming home, getting hugged by wives and kids. Very lovely scenes. Except for the man whose wife hit him with a mop, since he stopped to relax with some friends. But even that seemed nice and human, when seen from several hundred feet up. That's the greatest thing about being so high: the problems that you see below all look so manageable." Walter Water Snake sighed, at the memory of flying. "Birds have it best. They really do. However, after a delightful hour or so of sightseeing, The Delapidated Cloud and I—!

"Your flying machine? You called it that—?"

"Well, it had to have a name!"

"An' to think—I never knew!"

"Also, one woman had looked up and seen us. From her expression, I would guess that she thought we were some kind of migrating thing. And that she didn't want us to land in Hedley, and hoped that she'd never see us again. So, since she might have reported us to the Rare Bird Society, we decided we'd better get on with it, and made for the corner of Hedley Avenue and Upper Lebel Street, where the jail is. Of course all the windows have bars, but since it's summer and they've got no air-conditioning, the windows were open. The one we got in was in the lavatory. And the first cell we inspected held a man who'd been driving drunk. That was lucky, because I was on the floor now, and he thought I was just a bad dream. The second cell was occupied by a man who'd stolen a donut and was going to be held all night, without food. But the third cell— that was unoccupied. We knew who'd been in it, though. The officers had urged Mr. Budd to take a shower and change his clothes. They provided the clothes. But Mr. Budd's underwear was still on his bunk."

"Now comes the part I like," said Ashley. "I'm not partial to jails—"

"—but," Walter went on, "Mr. Budd was out by the sergeant's desk—*learning how to play poker!* And mostly dressed up in pieces of officers' uniforms. He had on Mike Gallagher's coat, and Mike was teaching him the difference between a flush and a straight. All the other cops were helping, too. Most of them had played in the meadow with Mike. Oh, and also—they'd sent out for pizza. My gosh!" Walter Water Snake leaped from the pool. "I *do* love Hedley! The dog-catchers all watch television, and the cops eat pizza and teach an old man to play poker! *Hooray!*" Walt flip-flopped joyously.

"Anyway—us birds and us snakes decided on this: Ashley warbled a little melody—and, as planned, Mr. Budd recognized the voice. He knew something was up. And then *I* was rearing up! Walter Water Snake! Me! I became a cobra! And it was very hard to do. I'm just not built to be vertical."

"A cobra snake?" gasped Chester.

"Darn right! One of my most disagreeable relatives!"

"But, Walter—how—?"

"How could I be a cobra? With no venom at all? And the tenderest heart in this whole meadow? I'll tell you how. The human beings come into this meadow—they

146

sit on benches, they read magazines, and sometimes they drop those magazines. One dropped magazine was all about science—with a reared-up cobra on the cover. I about passed out when I saw it—I can't stand nasty relatives!—but it served a purpose, that picture, when I imitated it in jail. But I've still got a pain in the neck where I tried to spread out—for realism. They rear and spread, cobras do. Makes me shiver to think about it."

"Oh, Walter!" said Chester. "How awful. Those poor policemen! Scared out of their wits—"

"I hated to do it," said Walter sadly—a bit too sadly.

"You loved to do it!" said Ashley. "Biggest night in your life!"

"Well, it served its purpose!" said Walt. "When the roaring cops took off—I did a fierce hiss, too—Mr. Budd just had to open the door. Ashley here conveyed the message that I was a friend—"

"—by sittin' on this cobra's head, an' singin' a familiar tune—"

"—and John Robin led the way. Until he got lost. The idiot! Then J.J. here took over. And this is a changed bird, let me tell you!"

"Now, Walt," said Ashley, "John did his own best—"

"You did more," J.J. voiced his trill again. "By singing on Abner's shoulder, on the way home, to make him have peace and have hope as we ran."

"Yes, but I was the lucky one. When everyone started to run, I thought—there goes the last of my tummy scales! I'll have to slither home. But Mr. Budd took a look at me—I think he may have recognized something —he opened his policeman's coat pocket—and in I jumped—"

"—and here we are!"

"Budd wasn't scared, though—!"

"At first he was—!"

"Not when you sang, Ashley. And I wasn't, either—!"

The tale was hurried to its end with the rushes and sudden interruptions of all the other animals.

TEN

A Meeting

"Someone's got to go get Dubber," said Chester. "Mr. Budd needs him."

"I will."

"No, me!" said J. J. Bluejay, who'd been listening with a new delight as Walter related all their adventures. "I never knew I had so much fun! Where is he?"

"Off near your beech," said Chester. "The TV viewers and pizza eaters just searched the near meadow."

J. J. Bluejay, with the gift of his wings, jumped up in the air. "Abner wants to see Dubber! We have got to get them together!" he announced from his perch of nothingness.

"The cabin may be watched secretly," said Chester.

"Even though there's no pizza or TV," Walt added.

J.J. jumped higher—then higher still: he could see upstream—and then settled down on Chester's log. "No one's there. They've given up. No one, I mean, except Mr. Budd. He's sitting on that stool of his, in the moonlight."

"Hush!"

A whistle was heard through the night. Then a call —"Dubber! Dubber!" Then nothing but shivering, whimpering sounds, like the sounds Dubber Dog might make himself. "They got you, too. I forgot. My dog. The same time as they captured me." In a while, the man who was crying fell silent.

"Mr. Budd's gone to sleep," said Walt. "All alone."

"I'm going to get Dubber," said J.J.

"Those guys may come back again—"

"No, they won't," Simon thought aloud. "Not tonight. Tomorrow maybe."

"Then tomorrow I'll peck their heads into the brook!" said the blue jay.

"And I'll become a cobra again!"

"And you'll both be killed!" said the cricket.

"Let's worry tomorrow," said Simon Turtle. "I've had enough worry these last two days to do for a lifetime."

"You folks go on up to the cabin," said J.J.

But Chester wondered, "Perhaps we shouldn't. I feel sort of embarrassed about watching Dubber and Mr. Budd meet."

"Me, too," said Walt. "But let's hurry, anyway. I can't stand the suspense!"

"Oh, me too then!" moaned Simon. "I'm too old to give up."

In silver moonlight and a flurry of silver-blue wings, J.J. flew off, to bring home a dog to his master. He felt good too, as he made his way through the trees, over open spaces, and at last saw the woods where Dubber was hiding.

J.J. alighted on his beech. The moon shone through the leaves beautifully, like a pure white flower that verged on the brink of its richest bloom. He was just about to squawk—"Aw! haw!"—but then he remembered his lessons from Ashley. He bobbed his head up and down, as if he were going to give out a "Doodly-oo" —and then he trilled. And his trills were getting better and better.

"Is that you, Ashley?" a blubbery voice asked, below.

"No, it's me!"

"Who's me?"

"J.J.!"

"I don't believe it!" Dubber Dog crept out from the shadow of the beech where he'd been in hiding, and looked up at the branches. "That voice was beautiful."

"Mine *is* now!" J.J. flickered down toward Dubber's voice, and found the dog. He had tried to conceal himself beneath last year's leaves and looked like a sad ghost of every October. "Hi, Dub! Old rub-a-dub-Dubber!"

"I know this is your beech," began Dubber nervously.

"And don't get nervous. I'm nice now." J.J. laughed his new laughter. "And I've got a surprise for you."

"What surprise?"

151

"You'll have to follow me and see!"

"*What* surprise—?"

"Well, goodbye now. I'm off to see if my surprise is still there." J.J. made as if to test his wings, getting ready for flight. " 'Course, this surprise may have woken up by now—"

"Is it Mr. Budd? Oh! Is Mr. Budd free—?"

"So long, D.D.," twittered J.J. "But someone's waiting for you or the cops. Whoever comes calling first." The blue jay flew away—very slowly, for a quick bird like J.J. He wanted to know he was being followed.

And he was. Dubber lumbered after him. In the dark, and in this part of the meadow, the dog might have gotten lost, if he hadn't had such a loving guide.

So back through the skeletal shadows of branches, trees, bushes the two friends went, toward Mr. Budd's cabin. J.J. darted ahead and waited patiently on a twig or a tuffet as Dubber caught up, noisily. The dog had never been known for his grace, and he was so eager now that his fumbling through the underbrush was clumsier than usual. It took quite a time to reach the cabin.

And while the teasing beneath the beech and the fumbling journey home took place, Chester, Simon, and Walt had been waiting. They'd come up the familiar path—then they'd seen Mr. Budd asleep on his stool, with his back propped against his home. The moonlight was making his gray hair look even more

A Meeting

silvery, as his head drooped on his chest. Now and then he'd fidget and say something, in his sleep. "Fisk!" he shouted once. And then mumbled, "Bad lettuce this year." And sighed. "New isinglass. I can't see the west, or Avon Mountain. Oh, Luke—I do miss you so much!" And then there was only more snoring.

"He's going to fall off that stool," said Walt.

"No, he's not," whispered Simon, in a voice that sounded very much like Mr. Budd's. "He's sat there as long as I've lived in my pool. And we've neither one of us lost our balance."

Everybody needed to talk—to fill up the space of expectancy—and the fear they felt at seeing this meeting.

"Hush now," said Chester. There was crashing in the underbrush. "I think it's Dubber—"

"It's either him or a dinosaur!" said Walter Water Snake.

Now, as Dubber appeared—J.J. flying above him— a muffled rumpus took place. No one wanted to wake up Mr. Budd, so the joy of everyone being free, not imprisoned by cops or dogcatchers, spread over everyone stealthily. Abner Budd stayed asleep, and wandered a long time in his dreams.

"Dubber—!"

"Walt—!"

"Welcome home—!"

"And Chester—!"

"Ha, dog—!"

"Our mockingbird, too! Gosh, I'm glad to be back! Just a day away seems like forever."

The hushed ruckus went on for several minutes, the hugging and greeting.

"And, Dubber," said Chester, "look up there—"

Asleep and snoring though he was, Mr. Budd somehow felt like the center of all the animals' happiness.

"He *is* back!" yelped Dubber. His eyes filled up. "You got him out, too. Oh, thanks, everybody! I don't know how to thank—"

"Then why try?" asked Chester briskly, and coughed. Sometimes feelings get too strong to be chirped.

"Did they hurt him in jail?"

"Not at all!" said Walt. "They gave him two desserts and one policeman's overcoat—and a lovely meal first. Meat loaf it was, and looked very tasty. But he wouldn't eat, so they left all the goodies in his cell and took him up to the head officer's desk."

"To punish him for not eating dinner?" asked Dubber.

"No—to teach him how to play poker." Walt went on and told the whole adventure over again. This was only the second time, and he hoped there were many more to come.

"I don't care about meat loaf!" Dubber erupted. "I just want to make sure that they treated him right. To think of it!—Abner Budd in *jail!*"

A Meeting

Walt wrapped himself around Dubber's neck. "Now listen to your old snakeskin collar—he's fine!"

"For now," said Simon.

"For now," echoed Chester.

"Look," said Ashley. "He's stirrin', up there."

Mr. Budd was mumbling something—the animals couldn't quite understand—it sounded like "Lived too long." Then he shifted positions on the stool, and fell into deep sleep again. Half the moonlight was blocked by the roof of his cabin. But part of his beard, as the moon eased away, was touched by the brilliance of the bright night.

"He's dreaming," said Dubber. "He dreams of the past. And the future he dreams might be."

"He was calling for you, earlier," said Chester Cricket.

"Me—?"

"Even when he knew you'd been taken away. And he tried to whistle, too."

"He always knew I loved that whistle. You know"— Dubber grinned, beneath his whiskers, and his eyes got shy—"we dogs do love to be whistled for."

"Then I guess he got tired. Who wouldn't? That long race from the jail—"

"He's waking up again!" Simon Turtle insisted. "I think his back hurts. Mine would, too—shell and all— if I'd leaned against that cabin so long."

"Dubber," said Chester—and his voice was firm,

ruthless almost. "This is up to you now. Go to him."

"Okay. But after today he'll probably just whop me again. I don't blame him."

The dog lumbered to Mr. Budd's feet. He took a look up. The man's face was working in dream-thoughts —just on the margin of waking up.

Then Dubber jumped: a big heave, but the dog accomplished it as gracefully as a cat.

"Who's that?" yelled Mr. Budd, thrown pell-mell from the end of his sleep.

Dubber whined in a voice that he knew his master would recognize.

"Why, Dubber—!"

A great big lapful of dog was nestling in Mr. Budd's arms.

"Oh, Dubber—it's you, it's you! You escaped, like me!"

Mr. Budd stroked Dubber's head. Then he scratched, because Dubber had twisted his neck: dogtalk for "Scratch me here, please." And this was a scratch in the back of the neck that Dubber had waited for for so long—this dog who had once only dreamed of ice cream.

"My dog," Mr. Budd kept saying. "I *am* so sorry I whopped you. And I kicked you, too, almost, that last day, when they took us away. My dog, my dog—my tomato dog—you're the best of the line. And I love you most. My little tomato pup." He lifted up Dubber's

head and kissed him on the short hairs of his nose.
"You're the best dog, Dubber."

Then Abner Budd began to cry.

"But, Dubber—I'm scared. I'm as scared as a little
boy."

Dubber licked his hands, to cheer him a little. But
nothing could help.

"I'm so scared!" sobbed Mr. Budd. "I'm old, and
nobody wants me at all." He fell back against the home
that he'd built. And his tears fell on Dubber's face.
"Oh, Dubber, Dubber—my dearest friend—whatever
will happen to both of us now?"

"I told you we shouldn't have watched," said
Chester. He jumped around so his back was to Mr.
Budd's cabin. His heart seemed to shrink and expand,
all at once. "I don't want to see things like this."

"Let's go back to the pool right now," said Simon.

On the way home, no one spoke.

But when they reached the little inlet where they
knew they'd be safe for the rest of their lives, Chester
Cricket blew up. When a cricket explodes—in anger
or despair—not too many humans hear about it. It is a
small rage, by the world's standards, but fierce.
Chester's friends could see him, and hear him,
trembling.

"I hate the world. I hate Hedley, Connecticut! I
hate everybody! And most of all I hate myself! There's
nothing that I can do—!"

A Meeting

"Now calm down, cricket," said Walt.

"*It's just not right!*—to throw a man out of his home that he built with his own hands—just because it doesn't look like a pizza parlor, all neon and junk, on Hedley Avenue!"

"Chester, if I may—!" Walt began.

"And they'll come! I know they'll come tomorrow! To get him. We have to *do* something! It was so much easier the last time. We only had to save the Old Meadow. Fool 'em into thinking that this place was historical. Well, Mr. Budd is historical. And human, too!"

"Chester—" Walter tried to begin again.

"And more! The field folk decided that we'd try to help. We decided that at the Great Debate. But not one person had an idea!"

"I've got one," said Simon. "Suppose we ask the people with teeth—like Frank Woodchuck—to dig holes around the cabin. Then the cops and the dog-catchers all would fall in, and—"

"That's ridiculous!"

Chester Cricket was not himself. No one ever had heard him shout like this. Everybody looked at everybody—Walt, Simon, J.J., Ashley—but nobody dared to say a word. Walt opened his mouth but snapped it shut: it wasn't the time, he decided.

"We *could* get the diggers to dig all around the cabin," said J.J. "Then Mr. Budd would be an island."

"You nutty bird!" squeaked Chester, in a cricket's

shout. "That's the silliest thing I've ever heard! What are woodchucks—and even *moles*—against tractors and bulldozers? They'd fill up any little moat like a beaver would dam up a stream."

"If I may suggest something—"

"*Tchoor!*" Chester turned on Walt. "You suggest all you want. But just remember that Mr. Budd is the soul of the whole Old Meadow. If they take him away —our hearts go, too."

Walter Water Snake had had enough. His tummy scales were still hurting, and although he had enjoyed his flight, his nerves were shot. "You crazy cricket! Now you shut up! I'll bite you in half! Just like a potato chip!"

"Folks—why don't we all relax?" sang Ashley. He'd learned, in his life in West Virginia, with coal miners especially, that a good tune sometimes could stop a fight. So he warbled a little ditty now.

It worked.

"Chester Cricket is right," said Walter Water Snake, and he spoke with extravagant dignity. "My crispy friend is often right." There was great dignity and respect in his voice, but also a little tooth of laughter began to make itself heard. "Mr. Budd *is* the heart and soul of this meadow of ours. We just need to make all the human beings see that. And if Mr. Budd was taken away—this meadow might just as well not exist."

"Hey, wait—"

A Meeting

"Chester Cricket," said Simon, "you have an idea. I can see it in your eyes."

Chester glanced at the mockingbird nervously. "You haven't been singing on the weather vane, Ashley."

"Y'all told me not to."

Chester Cricket went on to explain his scheme. And then twice more, since the first few times no one could believe their ears.

"That's asking a lot from all the field folk." Simon Turtle shook his head.

"It *is* the most outrageous thing I have ever heard!" said Walt.

"But y'all know somethin'—" Ashley whistled his courage up, at this great challenge. "It just might work —the good Lord willin'—"

"—*an' the creek don't rise!*" all the other animals joined in.

ELEVEN

The Old Meadow

It wasn't yet sunrise. But already a brightening ruddy glow came flaming through the feathery green of the willow trees that bordered the brook just before it rushed under the bridge beneath Mountain Road and left the Old Meadow forever. Almost all the human beings who lived in Hedley were still asleep—and so were most field folk. But not the birds. Those early risers were up and chirping to the new day, each other, themselves—anybody who'd listen.

"Lord, what a glory!" Ashley whistled his wonder. "We've been given a good day."

"The last," said Chester.

Both were sitting on the topmost ridge of Chester's log, and both were thinking of how far off the nighttime was, and oh what a day the mockingbird had ahead of him.

"It's an awful lot to ask," said the cricket. "Even of a person like you."

Ashley chose not to hear the implied compliment. "Dubber doin' what he's supposed to?"

The Old Meadow

"He's already woken up Mr. Budd and started to tug him by his pants. To the overgrown part. J.J.'s tugging his collar, and singing up some encouragement. They'll be safe there—"

"For today maybe," said Ashley. "One day."

"You don't *have* to, Ashley!" Chester burst out. "It's a crazy idea—!"

"Oh yes, I have to! What's more—I have to start right now." Ashley fluttered down and took a good big drink of brook water. "An' the Good Lord had *better* be *willin'!* He flew off toward his first tree. "Just hope the ol' throat don't give out!"

"Oh, and listen!" the cricket shouted after him. "The brook'll be here—if you need to moisten your throat, I mean." But Ashley had disappeared into the leaves of Bill Squirrel's maple. It wasn't as lofty as his elm, but he'd learned to make do.

"And I'll be here, too," murmured Chester Cricket helplessly. "Not that I'll do any good."

"Is he gone?" Walt's head appeared above the surface.

"Were you listening?"

"No! I could see it was private, between you two. But I was looking—from down below. I've been awake half the night."

"Yes, he's gone," said Chester. "Is Simon up?"

"Not on your life! Sleep first, disaster after—that's his motto. He's under your log, and just as asleep as a bear in December."

At that moment a carol of melody rang out of Bill's maple, which rose close to Mountain Road. A driver, who had to get up early and commute a long way to work, jammed on his brakes. His tires screamed. But the man had to hear that sound again.

"Well, it's started," said Chester.

"It's started," said Walt. "Meanwhile, you and I have got duties to do. I'm going to swim downstream and talk to Robert Rabbit. I'll send him back here. You hatched this plan. It's up to you to convince everyone."

"I wish I had a shell, like Simon."

"Too late now, creaky cricket! And I'll send up Frank Woodchuck, too. He swings a lot of weight with the bigger fur folk. And Donald—if he's on his twig—I'll tell him to come up toward noon. The insects are going to be awfully important!"

"You're telling me?" wailed Chester Cricket. "And here we're depending on one dragonfly! And a tetched one at that—tetched by sunlight, moonlight, the light of the stars—"

"—and the light in the eyes of his friends!" Walter splashed some water in Chester's face. "So cheer up—and chirp up!—Chester Cricket. This is the day when we field folk do or die for the sake of the one human being who loves us most."

Chester sat on his log as the early morning blossomed around him. For a while he just listened to Ashley sing.

And that helped a great deal. For inside himself he was summoning up all his strength and all his cricket's intelligence for the task that lay ahead of him: to persuade a whole meadow, with all its different animals, to act as if it were one living thing. His day would be almost as difficult as the mockingbird's, he thought.

Then he shook himself. No! The whole thing depended on Ashley. This day, Chester Cricket resolved, he wouldn't take any more thought for himself. He was just there to serve a mockingbird and a hopeless old man.

In a short while the field folk began to appear, routed out of their daily routines by Walter.

First came Frank Chuck and Robert Rabbit.

When he'd heard the scheme, Frank chewed it over with his big buck teeth. "And I can't even snore—?"

"Pretend to snore," said Chester Cricket. "Then afterwards you can snore for real."

Robert Rabbit took no convincing at all. "But I don't make noise," was all he objected.

"I've heard that rabbits scream, sometimes—"

"—just when we're unnerved," said Robert. "And a scream wouldn't be appropriate."

"You're right," said Chester. "I guess you'll just have to be quiet."

"Like fur I will! I'll beat my flat feet on that hollow log near my house—"

"Great!" said the cricket. "It'll sound like the drum in an orchestra."

The Old Meadow

The chipmunks, Emily and Henry, were a little reluctant at first. Then, when they'd talked it out with each other, they found that they both were excited—amazed! Emily was amazed, and Henry excited. They went home to their nook in the fallen-down stone wall where they lived and enjoyed their excitement—amazement—all day.

Chester Cricket was beginning to think that this day might not be so hard after all, when Donald Dragonfly flew up. Frank Chuck, Robert Rabbit, that crowd—they'd all been fairly cooperative, and Donald was—after all—an insect. As was Chester himself. He didn't anticipate problems. But he got them.

"Hi, Chister!" the dragonfly said, as he settled. His six wings took the sunlight and spread it all out on the pool. Light met water, and both exchanged hues. "What's up?"

"Donald—"

"I had the nicest thing this morning! One wing was dipping into the brook—and the other went up to the dawn, jist as I was waking up!"

"Donald, listen—there's something important—"

"That has niver happened to me before."

"*Donald!* You dope—! I didn't mean that." Chester touched a wing to Donald's wing: always a sign of peace, between insects. "But you have to listen! Because this is serious."

Donald tried to remember his wings' serious posi-

tions. They got scrambled. But finally they folded into something like a dragonfly's earnest attention. "Yis, Chister?"

"The thing is this—!" Chester Cricket explained the problem, and his own unlikely solution.

"No! Chister—*no!*" shouted Donald.

"This is a hard time—"

"Is it?" asked Donald. "I didn't know that." The dragonfly never thought of the world as a difficult place. The news that it was came as an unwelcome surprise. "I thought times were good, not hard." He lifted his wings and peeped, "I thought times were *grand!* It's August, Chister, and you know what that means: *insect time!* Oh-boy-oh-boy-oh-boy! You loud ones git to make your noises—and I git to shine my best!"

Chester loved Donald dearly, but he never knew whether to talk to him seriously—bug to bug—or just laugh his antennae off. "Now, Donald"—he touched one of Donald's wings with a wing—"we have a problem. Mr. Budd's in a fix." Chester patiently went over —and over—and *over*—Mr. Budd's trouble. Each time, though, Donald understood a bit more. But unless a discussion was all about light, Donald hardly ever remembered it. "Has Mr. Budd ever hurt any one of you dragonflies—?"

"No—"

"Or killed a firefly—?"

"No. I knew one named Pete who sat on his

shoulder, and Mr. Budd didn't stir a hair. So's not to scare Pete."

"Well, all *right*, then!" said Chester. "You have *got* to contact the cicadas and katydids. All those critters that make August August. And the fireflies, too, who still can blink—it's been a wet summer—there must be some, even if their time is earlier. You have *got* to get the insects all ready!"

"Oh, all right. It won't hurt me—though I do like to go to sleep early. Unliss disturbed. And I'm not oftin disturbed. But the night fliers, Chester—and the night chirpers too, like yourself—*and the full moon is tonight!* I forgot!"

"It'll just be a little time," said Chester. "And then—" He went over the plan once more.

"But there's hundrids and hundrids of us," said Donald. "I can't link antennae with every one!"

"You don't need to. Just touch ten and tell them to get the message spread. By nightfall every insect in the meadow will know."

"Okay," said Donald, doubtfully.

"And, Donald," said Chester with a lot of confidence —to reassure his friend, "this is going to be the great night in your life."

"Oh! I didn't know that!" Donald suddenly believed. And hurried off through the morning air to do his task. Which was only to mobilize every insect in the whole meadow. Donald couldn't fly without showering colors all around. But he just took glory for granted.

"If it isn't your greatest night," said Chester Cricket to himself, "it'll be my fault—not yours."

The cricket was thinking of responsibility, the leaden weight of it, like a thunderhead, when J.J. alighted beside him.

"I've got them hidden. There's a stretch of grass behind a bramble—poor Abner was so tired this morning, we woke him up early—but Dubber and him are sleeping there. Dubber knows to keep him quiet, too, when he wakes up, until tonight."

"You've been great—" began Chester.

"Y'all don't know how great! I've got all the birds in line, too! Took a little bit of persuading—since all of them think you're crazy. But even the sparrows came around."

"I'm sure," said Chester. "Poor things! They're probably all black and blue—"

"When you bash them, sparrows don't get black and blue," J. J. Bluejay explained. "Their feathers just fall off. But I've done with those tactics. I was sweet and—kind and reasonable. And all the birds were so amazed that J. J. Bluejay was sweet and kind and reasonable—they all agreed to everything! How about that? And even—they all agreed to staying up *late!* All night, if necessary. And we like to turn in early."

"Donald said the same thing."

"But we'll be up! Or else this meadow will be littered with feathers! Tomorrow morning. And listen now, Chester—" J.J. treated himself to a trill. "I got the *Hawk* to cooperate—"

"I don't believe it!"

"When all the little chirpies had agreed—John Robin helped a lot, too—I decided, why not? I had the grackles under my wing, those bums! Why not try for the highest bird. So I flew!"

J.J. choked at the great experience. It was probably the highest point in his life. "I got higher than I'd ever been before. Then the Hawk was there! He was amazed that I'd gotten so far up. We talked on the wind. He was still puzzled that I could fly so high—so was I!—and He said, 'What in the name of thunder and lightning are you doing up here?' I explained—and He shrieked. And what He was shrieking was '*Me*—?' 'Just once,' I explained. 'And if you do—I'll teach you to sing—' " J.J. fumbled for his voice. "He knew that I'd made a fool of myself. But instead of knocking me down to earth, He just laughed. And He said He'd shriek. Swoop, too."

"The Hawk! Wow!" said Chester. "Someone has to tell Ashley—"

"I will," said J.J. "He's got to take a break between songs."

"That's the trouble," said Chester. He looked up at Bill Squirrel's maple. "He's got to sing all day. Find a quiet song—and then whisper to him about the Hawk.

And the time. He'll understand. Great birds always recognize one another."

"So far, so good."

It was almost noon, and J. J. Bluejay had flown back to the log. He'd been following Ashley all morning, since he got back from the wild part, mostly to keep him informed of the progress of the plan, but also to give him encouragement and keep him company. Once Ashley had darted down himself, to take a drink and have a gargle, but he hadn't said a single word. Everyone knew he was saving his voice.

"Where is he now?" asked Chester.

"Up toward the reservoir. He stopped fifty cars this morning, on Mountain Road, and decided he'd better move on."

"That's what we decided last night," said Chester. "That he'd move around. It's safer for Ashley, too."

"I hope those cars get gridlocked!" Walt snapped his tail like a whip.

"What's a gridlock?!" asked J.J.

"Ask Chester. He's lived in New York."

"It's when cars get all packed together so tight that not one of them can move. The human beings all swear and shout, and honk their horns—"

"—and serves them right!" said Walt.

"One funny thing did happen, though," J.J. laughed. "On the way to the reservoir Ashley perched on Mr.

Budd's weather vane. Not for long! Don't look so con-
cerned now, cricket. He knows what we're saving that
for. But he sang a while—and 'ol' Malvina heard him.
She made her boys carry her favorite armchair all the
way out to the edge of the brook. And it is big! But
there she sits, even though the mockingbird has moved
on. She hears him faintly—and that's enough."

J.J. reverted to an "awk! squawk!" laugh. "And she
said, 'I'm so glad that you two didn't catch him!' 'But
Grandma,' says Alvin, 'it was your idea!' 'Hush, child,'
Malvina says grandly, 'and listen to beauty. But before
you do—go get my footstool.'"

The animals took a long laugh at that; it broke the
tension of the day.

"And then," J.J. went on, since he was as nervous
as all the rest, "she made one of her sons get a saucer
of real corn kernels! Not corn candy."

"Did Ashley eat some?" asked Chester.

"No. I thought they might give him strength, but he
just shook his head and said, 'Don't sing well on a full
belly, J.J.'"

"That Ashley—" Walt shook his head, in awe. "He's
a wonder—"

"Hush! Listen! There he goes," said the blue jay.

In the distance, a far-off song seemed to float to the
north. "He's heading for the wild part."

"Not too near, I hope!" said Chester. "That's where
Dubber and Mr. Budd are hidden."

"Oh, no," said J.J. "But he told me he needs to sing on every side. He has to turn this Old Meadow into a magnet made of music. So the humans will all be drawn to it everywhere. The Hawk's hidden somewhere up there, too—"

"The Hawk—! Already?"

"I think so. He heard the singing way up in the sky, and came down to hear it clearer. I saw a shape, falling," said J.J. "But I'm not sure. Don't worry, though, Chester. Tonight he'll do what He promised He would."

"I hope!" said Chester.

No one spoke. In the silence, their ears could get sharp. They all followed the mockingbird's traveling song.

All day he'd been singing, from tree to tree, never lingering long in one place. But what all the field folk didn't know—he was singing of *them*. Some suspected —like Chester—even though they weren't sure. His first joyous greeting, from Bill Squirrel's maple, had been for the summer day itself. But after that carefree serenade, the mockingbird had to think of *things*. Sometimes Ashley made up a melody just for melody's sake, but most often a mockingbird thinks of things. Not necessarily all the things that his voice imitates: sometimes he need only think of—a tree, say, or a daisy, or rapids where a stream runs on under the sun. He needn't be seeing or hearing them now, just only imagining them. Faced with all those hours that he knew he had to fill with music, Ashley summoned up thoughts of the world he knew and the worlds he'd only dreamed about.

But since there he was in the midst of the Old Meadow, he decided to start with the friends he had there. In a rippling little ditty Henry and Emily Chipmunk were discussing whether to bite their lawn—that's how they mowed it—or polish the white stones that formed their front walk. A fanfare, which Ashley announced around ten o'clock in the morning, lead into a solemn parade: Bea Pheasant, followed by her mate, was strutting past Tuffet Towers, her home. And at high noon, as a special present that he knew would not be received, when the sun was dazzling everyone, Ashley sang a song about the light on Donald's wings and the colors they cast on Simon's Pool. Of course Donald didn't understand, although he did hear. He was too busy rousing fireflies—they do get tired in August—and telling them they had one more job to do.

Donald Dragonfly didn't understand that this song was for him, and neither did the human beings who heard it. But they all knew, the people who screeched to a halt on the roads surrounding the meadow, that something strange—a few called it "unnerving"—was happening in this quaint little space, grass, flowers, trees, that had been declared "A monument" amid concrete and brick.

The Old Meadow

On the local radio station, a diligent announcer kept commenting on Ashley: at nine in the morning, the early news, he was "an unusual event"—by noon he was "something very special"—and by three in the afternoon "a miraculous phenomenon!" Word spread among the human beings almost as fast as among the insects that Donald Dragonfly kept stirring up.

By four o'clock, cars started to block one another. The drivers first honked, and then got out to shout at anyone who was handy. The gridlock built, all during the evening.

It wasn't evening that Ashley feared. Or Chester Cricket, on his log. His antennae twitched at the sounds all around—brakes, doors slamming, voices arguing—but they were the daytime human noises. It was the night Chester Cricket dreaded—and Ashley, too, as he sang. This night. When the Meadow saved Mr. Budd—or all the field folk failed together.

Then the August darkness finally was there. The human beings, clustered around the Old Meadow, were full of wonder at Ashley's song. And the animals, clustered within green boundaries, were full of fear—could Ashley's song work? The full moon rose in the southeast sky, silvering the green willow trees. It was neither worried nor wondering. For itself the full moon was only fulfilled, like a wish come true.

The human beings were watching the moon, too. But few of them suspected what Chester Cricket could hear: that as the moon rode higher and higher, the mockingbird was working its light artfully into his song. Still, some people had the cloudy thought, somewhere in their minds, that the light of a full moon and a mockingbird's singing might both be part of one single day.

Ashley had circled the meadow five times, in the course of the hours, perching here, perching there, but always careful to avoid the same trees. Now, however, he decided that this was the time to return to Bill Squirrel's maple. The largest crowd of human beings was gathered there, and Ashley knew that, for better or worse, the final moments of this day were approaching.

First he needed a drink. From a willow tree beside the bridge he flew to Simon's Pool. In the darkness, his fluttering arrival surprised everyone.

"Time's gett'n' near."

"Ashley Mockingbird," began Chester Cricket, "you are a wonder!"

"Yup. The ol' throat's holdin' up. So far."

"You get better and better! How *do* you do it?"

"When the voice is workin', I think it's better not to question it." Ashley took his drink. Then looked up at the sky. "Sure is a lovely night. Just so balmy an' beautiful. Reminds me of West Virginia—"

"I wish it was absolutely black!" said Chester. "That's what we need. Complete darkness."

"May get your wish," said the mockingbird. "Look yonder—in the west. Those big clouds still are gatherin'.'' He took a second drink and sloshed it around in his throat. "Has somebody fetched Mr. Budd and Dubber?"

"I got them as soon as the night settled in," said J.J.

"The whole day's a bust, if Abner's not here."

"They're back in the cabin," the blue jay explained. "Keeping very quiet! Mr. Budd doesn't know what's happening—but he sure knows that *something* is!"

Ashley glanced up and searched the night sky. "If that Hawk now just sticks to his word—"

"Look! There He is!" whispered Walt.

A black shape hovered against the moon—then slowly edged out of the shining white face. Chester knew that the Hawk was circling, for stars disappeared, momentarily, as he blotted them out in his flight.

"I'd like to meet him," murmured Ashley. "A wonderful flyer. He lives so high."

"No one knows the Hawk," said Chester. "Not even the ones who have talked to Him."

"Well—back to work! Here I go—"

"Good luck!" Chester shouted.

"Good luck to all of us!" added Walter Water Snake.

Ashley flew to the maple. His song this time was all about Simon's Pool—and Simon and Walter and Chester Cricket. He'd been saving them up, all day; for one of his most important melodies. And all the while he kept an eye cocked toward the west, where rising black clouds were canceling stars.

Simon's rhythm, in the song, was sort of plodding,

slow but sure. Walter has a slithery tune. It was beautiful, but teasing, too. Chester got four chirps—and
Ashley imitated him exactly—but they formed a music
that pierced the hearts of the human beings, the
animals too, whoever heard it.

Those clouds reached the moon. The sky was now
black.

"Oh, now!" Chester Cricket said to himself. "If ever
—now!"

The Hawk couldn't have heard him. Perhaps he felt
Chester's urgent wish. For high up in the sky a scream
was heard—a terrible shriek, which felt like a threat
to everyone. Down it plunged, that sound, until animals
and human beings blocked their ears. The August sky
was filled with terror.

"He did it!" said Chester, to himself.

Ashley broke off his song in mid-melody.

And the Old Meadow vanished.

The scream that fell down from the sky and the
silence of the mockingbird were the signal for the
world to end.

It was utterly dark, and when Ashley stopped singing, the jubilant sounds of summer died. The happy,
confused din of insects and the rustling of the animals
failed. There was little wind, but it, too, seemed to fall
still. Or did Chester only imagine this? The brook,
too—there was no silencing it—but a living stream
hushed its rapids and eddies. And the cricket didn't
imagine that.

The Old Meadow

No human being dared to speak, and no animal would. In the cars lined up on Mountain Road, where men and women had been chatting, happy—some kids had been crying, because they were tired—all around the Old Meadow the human beings seemed frozen with fear.

For this was the dreadful and endless dark that filled the enormous emptiness—which was all there was— before the heavens and earth appeared.

Ashley stiffened himself for several minutes, in Bill Squirrel's maple. He wanted the human beings to know what this silence and this darkness felt like. Then soundlessly he flew down to Mr. Budd's cabin. He'd memorized the way. Flew in through the open door, and perched on Abner's only table. Abner always kept a candle there. Ashley made the softest chirp he could.

The man and his dog had been outside, amazed and marveling—like everyone else. But Mr. Budd knew that voice. "Is it you, my friend?"

"Chirp!"

Mr. Budd went inside. "Do you want a little light! Is that it?"

"Chirp."

"Well, all right, then. But for me—I'm not scared of the dark. At least not tonight."

"Chirp."

Mr. Budd found his matches and lit the candle.

Those human beings who were in a position to see

the cabin first saw a single bright spark shine out. Then a steady thread of light appeared. The fate of the meadow—not only the meadow—the future of the whole world seemed to hang from this filament of light that shone through the cracked glassine window of an old man's ramshackle cabin.

Ashley stayed by the candle a while and let the light shine on his feathers. Then he flew through the door and up to his proper perch: Mr. Budd's weather vane.

He waited there, for a couple of seconds. So much, he knew, depended on him. He took the deepest breath of his life—and sang a scale. In a voice that no mockingbird had ever had to use before, both beautiful and powerful, his sound raced from high to low. Then reversed. Up. *Up!* His voice went from low to high. Then he sang about Mr. Budd, and his years in the meadow, his loneliness and his happiness there—his age and his youth. And not one soul understood that song—not even Mr. Budd.

"Now! Now!" whispered Chester to Donald.

The dragonfly flew off.

"Me, too," said J.J. "And they'd better be awake!" He, too, flew away.

Fireflies, like children with sparklers on the Fourth of July, came alive beside the brook. When the woodchuck saw life was possible, he began to belly-laugh. Robert Rabbit beat his left foot on a tree trunk. And underground, Paul Mole sang the song of the earth.

Chester Cricket sang, too—all the songs, both animal and human, that he could remember.

Some insects simply banged their antennae together, and hoped that the sound would be heard. Most thrilling of all—in the dead of this night, all the birds of the meadow began to sing.

Far above, the clouds lifted from the moon, like a veil lifting off of a human face. And the Hawk, who had one sweet note in his voice, as well as a scream, sang it over and over, as he circled around. Perhaps he, too, had been taking singing lessons.

The human beings breathed again. And the world was remade.

There *was* gridlock in Hedley that night. But as the cars and the human beings extricated themselves, not one person dared to honk a horn.

TWELVE

Avon Mountain

"There he comes again!"

Walter Water Snake was a very different snake than the one who'd grumbled at Dubber's arrival a short few weeks before. He also knew he'd be greeting a very different dog.

"Hi, Walt!" Dubber Dog lumbered up and settled himself on the bank. There was a single tuffet there that made a great backrest. "Hi, Chester! Hi, everybody! Can I join y'all?"

"*Tchoor!*"

Everybody—a squirrel, a robin, a rabbit, one turtle, one cricket—said, "Hi!"

"Am I part of everybody?" asked Donald Dragonfly hopefully, in his crackly, uncertain voice.

"You sure are! You dashing dragonfly!" Walt was feeling expansive. Not expansive in his neck, as in his cobra impersonation at the Hedley Police Station, but his heart was expanded with happiness.

"Me? Dashing?" Donald rasped his laugh, which

sounded as if someone using sandpaper had just come down with the hiccups. *"K! k! k!"*

"How is the Grand Old Man of the meadow?" Walt asked Dubber.

"The Grand Old Man—" Now Dubber laughed. And his laughter sounded like someone's stomach who'd had too much to eat. "The Grand Old Man is as mad as a hornet!"

"I once—" began Donald.

"When wasn't he?" interrupted Simon, whose memory was as long as Abner's.

"The old gaffer! They're letting him stay. He ought to be grateful!"

"Don't you call him that, Walter! He's not an 'old gaffer'!"

"I meant it in the very best way." Walter apologized grandly, by bowing in the brook.

To prove that all he had said was true, he whipped himself up and became a dog collar—once more—around Dubber Dog's neck. Since the trip from the dog pound, poor Dubber had never known when to expect this playful and loving behavior from Walt.

"Am I chokin' you?"

"Yes!"

"Har! har!" Walter loosened his grip and dropped down on the meadow grass. It felt almost as cool and smooth as the waters in Simon's Pool. "So the Grand Old Gaffer's as mad as a hornet."

"I once knew a hornet who *niver* got mad!" mused

184

Avon Mountain

Donald Dragonfly, all by himself in his thoughts somewhere. "His name was James." He thought about this
peaceable hornet for as long as he could remember to
think—at least a minute. "I wonder where James is
now." Then the yellow of a passing butterfly's wing set
him thinking about the sun. And that was Donald's
favorite topic for thought.

"What's he mad at?" asked Walt.

"The Town Council's not only letting him stay.
They're putting in plumbing and electricity!"

"Oh!" moaned Walter Water Snake. "Can things
get any worse?" Then he started to laugh, and slipped
over the bank and into the water.

"They almost wanted to put in gas!" said Dubber.
"For a brand-new stove. But Abner—in my heart I call
him 'Abner' now—said he'd burn down his house if
they did. So it's going to be an electric stove."

"We didn't know things had gone that far," said
Chester.

"They went that far the day after Dark Night. The
Town Council met—whoever does run it—and while
whoever was making up everybody's minds, the Irvins
roared in, Malvina at the head of them. Of course
they'd been out on Dark Night and all of them realized
how much Mr. Budd meant to everything, and Malvina
demanded that he be protected—as if Abner was a
mountain or valley. Anyway—'Something *natural!*'
she screamed. '*He cannot be replaced!*' One son suggested he be 'an endangered species,' but nobody cared

for that. If one lonely old man was an endangered species—then everyone is. They decided to spruce up the cabin—mostly, I think, just to get Malvina out of the room." Dubber sighed. "And, given Malvina—I think I'd agree to anything, too."

"Anyway," he went on, "they're putting in plumbing, electricity. And the fights have been avoided so far. We had a near one, though. One plumber stepped on a squash. The foreman had to offer Abner a lettuce-and-tomato sandwich—or else there'd have been a brawl. Of course, Abner would have lost. Because the plumber was husky and young, and ready to take offense. But they shared a sandwich, and tempers cooled."

Dubber Dog reflected. "Like an ornery bulldog, that plumber was. But I guess Abner, too, must have been like that—feisty—when he was young. Anyway, it's all right now. Except Abner said, 'If they tear up one tomato plant—or one string bean—watch out!' "

"Here he comes!" said Walter Water Snake. "And he hardly ever comes down to the pool."

A lumbering was heard upstream.

"I came down myself," said Dubber Dog, " 'cause I did not like to hear Abner use awful words to the workmen. You've got to be nice if he swears a little."

"Is swearing like—swearing to keep a promise?" asked Donald Dragonfly.

Mr. Budd lunged through thickets, shrubs, and bulrushes. "Where are you, dog—!" He broke through a patch of vines. "Oh, *there* you are—you Dubber you! My mutt—!"

There was that one tuffet that grew on the bank above Simon's Pool. It seemed like a seat—an empty throne. Abner Budd sat on it. "Got lots of friends here, too, don't you, dog?" Mr. Budd looked at all the animals—who were not afraid, and didn't hide.

"I'm ready to give up," said Abner. "Come here, Dubber—"

The dog jumped up in Abner's lap—that was happening more often now—and Abner stroked his head.

"It's not only plumbing and the electricity—they're insulating my cabin now! Why, I don't need insulation! Comes a cold night in February—I just put on two or three burlap blankets. You'll lie beside me. I get to the spring. At least—I always have. So far. Perhaps we should go to Maine. They may not have 'improvements' there."

Dubber slipped off Mr. Budd's lap. He could see that his master was tired. And Abner eased off the tuffet. He rolled up his trousers, "These knees are hurtin' again." Abner Budd lay back and looked up at Bill Squirrel's maple. Its green had reddened, the last few days. "Why, I didn't know it was so near fall!" Abner mumbled something important about the fall, but no one could understand what he said. Then he fell asleep.

Dubber looked up sadly. "I guess he'll be falling

asleep more and more." He was thinking of hours of loneliness, while he waited, as Mr. Budd slept. Then he stopped feeling sorry for himself. "All you guys here have to help me take care of him—!"

"We will," said Chester. "And we'll all keep both of you company, too."

"We'll never leave, though," said Dubber.

In a silent reverie, the cricket was thinking—On Dark Night the insects seemed like the heart of the meadow. Now Mr. Budd and Dubber are. I guess the Meadow has many hearts. Chester hoped that he was one, too.

A hurrying of wings was heard in the air above the animals.

"Just had to have one last look around. With my virtuoso friend here."

"Mm!" grumbled Walt. " 'One last look—' I don't like the sound of that."

"Now, don't go on. I told you right from the start that I had responsibilities, back in West Virginia. An' J.J.'ll guard y'all—with a squawk or a trill—whatever he feels like makin' that day, if somebody bad shows up. Like a kid with rocks or two men with butterfly nets. Funny, though," the mockingbird thought, "that family turned out to be the Old Meadow's best protection." He whistled happily.

But his laughter didn't work.

He'd meant to soothe all his friends' disquiet. The

field folk didn't make a sound. They all fidgeted nervously and didn't dare even glance at each other from the corner of worried eyes.

"Now don't y'all do that!" hollered Ashley—and tried to make his mockingbird's voice sound ugly. But couldn't. "Don't you dare to be miserable—!"

"But you'll wait a while—" said Chester Cricket anxiously. He looked upwards, as if expecting something. "A week—or a couple of days—"

"Right now!" said Ashley.

"No—later," pleaded Dubber Dog.

"This very second," the mockingbird said. "It's no use to make it worse—"

The field folk fell still. No one had a word to say.

But Walter Water Snake wouldn't let this miserable silence go on. "Ashley—can I recite something? Just a little jingle that I composed."

"Tchoor, Walt!" Ashley wouldn't stop trying to cheer folks up.

"I composed this quite a while ago." No one had seen Walt so upset before, almost tongue-tied—and for such a great talker, too. "I hadn't made up my mind— that is—if you might like to hear—or if I should just forget the whole thing—and—"

"I'm sure he'd like to hear!" said Chester, still searching the sky.

"You got somethin' to say?" Ashley asked.

"I think I do—"

"Then say it, snake! We've been up in the sky together, you and I."

Walt's voice was freed, and he blurted out:

A mockingbird with a golden throat
Flew out of the South, flew he.
We stopped—we wondered—each glorious note!—
We listened most gratefully.

In embarrassment Walt ducked to a deep depth of the pool where he could feel safe. Then curiosity overcame him. His eyes—just his eyes—appeared. Then his head! "You hated it, didn't you?" he asked, in a poet's agony.

"Walter Water Snake," said Ashley, and his voice was somewhat husky now, "that was beautiful! I don't deserve it—but it was beautiful, anyway."

"Oh, yes, it was!" shouted Chester Cricket frantically. "It was—why—" He started to chirp as loud as he could.

"Have you gone off your antennae?" said Walt. "What's *wrong* with you—?"

"Ashley!" begged Chester Cricket. "Please sing those up-and-downs, like you did on Dark Night—"

Without understanding why Chester had asked, the mockingbird sang his scales.

In the sky a shape that had wings was seen falling in lofty spirals, down to the earth. It seemed to the field folk as if Mr. Budd's iron weather vane had taken on life and was flying to them.

"Thank goodness!—He heard!" said Chester Cricket. "He came here last night and made me promise I'd let Him know when Ashley was going to leave."

In a moment, the Hawk was perched beside Chester. His feathers were somewhat dull in their color, but his eyes were fierce and bright, and His beak—that sharp beak—could have picked apart any soul in the whole Old Meadow. No one had seen Him this close up before, and no one could dare to look at Him for long. With rapid movements of His head, he jerked His eyes off one animal and fixed his glare on another.

Then, having examined them all, He pointed his gaze at Ashley.

"I'm—most proud to meet you, Hawk." And even the mockingbird's voice failed him now. He was just as stuttery and embarrassed as Walter Water Snake had been. "I've been wantin' to thank you for Dark Night. Your scream is what did it."

The Hawk lifted His enormous wings. They were powerful as the wind, expanded. He began a shriek— but then muffled it. All knew what He was saying was "No!" He made the melancholy sound that He'd made on Dark Night, when the world reappeared—melancholy and beautiful. All knew He was saying: "You made it happen." His wings settled against Him again.

Still flustered, Ashley tried to ask, "Is there somethin' you'd like, Hawk?"

The great bird stared.

191

Avon Mountain

"I was just about to tell my friends here—someday I'll be back. They'll see a little black speck come flyin' over Avon Mountain—an' it'll be me!"

The Hawk ruffled his feathers. He looked at Ashley with eyes that held love and amusement both. "Avon Mountain is my home," he said, in his muffled thunder. "I'll see you first. And I'll conduct you here. Now sing for me!"

"Y'all want a song? Okay—!" The mockingbird flew to Mr. Budd's tuffet and perched beside his head. "I don't think I'll wake him up. Some human bein's hear best asleep."

Ashley started to sing. This song was not about the Old Meadow. Or even about Connecticut. It was all about West Virginia and his people—"our people," he always called them—Hank and Ella and the kids, and all the others who awaited him there. It was all about hollers that few human beings had ever seen. And pools in the hollers that no human being had seen at all. And the mountains in the distance, where blue mountains blended into blue sky, with no break between them at all.

The singing grew so sweet and real—and difficult to bear—that all who were there had to close their eyes.

In shreds of sound, the voice trailed off.

And when, eyes brimming, the animals dared to see again, the mockingbird, along with his song, had flown away.